Grave-robbing wasn't exactly in
Mike Shayne's line . . . especially the
grave of someone's now deceased pet.
And the demise of a Pekinese doesn't
seem particularly important. But
when death is caused by strychnine . . .
obviously intended for someone far
more important than a pooch . . .
grave-robbing begins to seem more
reasonable. So Mike went fishing
on Biscayne Bay—with Tim Rourke for
rowing, two poles for fishing, and a
shovel for digging up death.

Die Like A Dog

**BRETT
HALLIDAY**

A DELL MYSTERY

Published by
DELL PUBLISHING CO., INC.
750 Third Avenue
New York 17, N.Y.

© Copyright 1959 by Brett Halliday

Dell ® TM 681510, Dell Publishing Co., Inc.

Reprinted by arrangement with the author

Designed and produced by
Western Printing and Lithographing Company

Dedication: For CHLOE

Previous Dell Edition #D391

New Dell Edition:
First Printing—April, 1967

Printed in U.S.A.

Chapter one

There was a quizzical smile on Lucy Hamilton's lips and a little dancing light in her brown eyes as she opened the door to her employer's private office and announced demurely, "There is a lady to see you, Mr. Shayne."

It was a warm Miami morning, and Michael Shayne was slumped in a swivel chair behind his wide desk in shirt-sleeves, with collar unbuttoned and tie awry. In front of him was an open checkbook, a pile of canceled checks and the monthly bank statement. His left hand clawed through unruly red hair and his right hand reached out automatically for a pair of nested paper cups beside the bank statement as he arched ragged brows at his secretary and growled, "A lady?" in a tone of disbelief.

Lucy nodded firmly and drew the door shut behind her. She advanced toward him, saying in an altered tone, "Ditch that brandy, Michael, before I bring her in, and for heaven's sake, straighten your tie. You might even slip on a jacket for once."

"Why should I ditch a drink?" Shayne lifted the twin cups and sipped from the contents.

"All right," said Lucy in a tone of forbearance. "Down the hatch with it and get rid of the evidence. I'm very sure that Miss Henrietta Rogell is *not* one to approve of drinking at eleven o'clock in the morning." She reached his side and bent down to brush a coarse lock of red hair back from his forehead.

Shayne grinned up at her and protested, "I didn't know we were interested in Miss Henrietta Rogell's approval or disapproval."

"But we are, Michael. She's the first client in two weeks." She slid around behind his chair and put her arms around each side of his neck to button his collar and straighten his tie.

"We're doing all right without any clients. I've been going over last month's bank statement . . ."

"And there is less than two thousand dollars in our checking account," Lucy interrupted him. She stepped back to survey his appearance with a nod of approval. "Miss Henrietta is John Rogell's sister . . . and only living relative."

"The millionaire who died a couple of days ago." Shayne shrugged and tossed off the rest of his cognac. He crumpled the cups in a big fist and dropped them into a wastebasket, then closed the checkbook and shoved it aside. "All right, Miss Hamilton. Show her in."

Shayne got to his feet behind the desk when Lucy ushered the prospective client into his office a few moments later. Miss Rogell looked to be a tough seventy. She was tall and angular, and had a seamed face that had the color and appearance of old leather. Brown hair that was liberally streaked with gray was drawn back tightly from her face into an untidy bun. She wore a gray silk suit with pleated skirt, and loose jacket that hung awkwardly from bony shoulders. Expensive white silk gloves were incongruous below brown and sinewy bare forearms. Service-weight hose accentuated thick calves, and her shoes were sturdy brown oxfords that were probably hand-crafted.

Lucy said, "This is Miss Henrietta Rogell, Mr. Shayne," and went out, closing the door to the private office.

Shayne blandly inclined his head and motioned to an upholstered armchair beside his desk. "Won't you have a seat, Miss Rogell?"

She strode forward, flat-footed, and said, "Of course I'll have a seat, young man. You don't expect me to remain standing, do you? I expect this to be quite a lengthy interview." Her voice matched her appearance. It was strong and deep without being harsh or masculine. She lowered herself solidly into the chair and planted both feet flat in front of her with knees together.

"Now then, before I waste any more of my time, I want to know exactly what your charges are."

Shayne sat down in his swivel chair and leaned back comfortably. "My charges for what?"

"For whatever you do. Detecting, of course. You do call yourself a detective, I believe."

Shayne said gravely, "I am a detective, Miss Rogell. Licensed by the state of Florida to practice that profession. Tell me your problem and we can discuss the fee later."

She said, "Nonsense. I'm too old to buy a pig in a poke. Let's have it understood from the beginning so there'll be no outrageous bill for me to pay at the end. Exactly what do you consider your time worth?"

Shayne got a pack of cigarettes from his shirt pocket and lit one. He blew out the match with a stream of smoke and said, "That depends entirely on what I am able to do for you. I think you've come to the wrong office, Miss Rogell," he went on briskly before she could speak. "My secretary can give you a list of half a dozen competent detectives who will quote you a flat daily rate for their services . . . plus expenses . . . and they won't pad the expense account too heavily. I think you'd be happier with one of them."

Her eyes were very clear and very blue. They remained unwinkingly fixed on his face as he spoke and her leathery face showed no trace of expression.

"You have no regular rate of charges?"

Shayne blandly expelled smoke from both nostrils and shook his head. "No more so than a self-respecting attorney has."

"What assurance do I have that you won't accept my case and then gouge me for some fantastic amount after doing nothing to earn it?"

Shayne said, "You have no assurance at all, Miss Rogell, that I won't do exactly that." He put his hands flat on the desk in front of him and half rose from his chair. "My secretary will give you that list of names on your way out."

She remained firmly seated and said, "Humph. I like plain speaking, young man. I'm a plain-spoken person myself. I want you to prove that my brother was murdered and to see that the person or persons responsible are made to pay for the crime."

Shayne hesitated, narrowing his eyes thoughtfully, and then sank back into his chair. "I understood from the newspapers that your brother died of a heart attack."

"Of course. That's what they called it. But I know John was poisoned."

"How do you know?"

"Because I have eyes to see what's going on, and a brain to add two and two together. If I had the proof I wouldn't be here in your office, obviously. That's what I'm hiring you for."

Shayne said, "Murder is a matter for the police, Miss Rogell. Have you discussed your suspicions with them?"

"Do I look like a complete nincompoop? Of course I

have. I called the police immediately after John died, and the two detectives who came just listened to me politely and promised they would investigate. Investigate?" Her upper lip curled bitterly over the word. "They asked a few questions of the very people who fed John the poison, and then went away saying they would file a report."

"Did they?"

"I suppose they did, and I'd give a great deal to see just what sort of report they filed. I think it's my right to see it, and I demanded a look at it from Chief Gentry just an hour ago. I'm a taxpayer, I told him, and my taxes help pay your salary and your entire force. But he beat around the bush and said the matter was closed. He refuses to order an autopsy even after I told him about the attempt on my own life last night. He thinks there must be some mistake . . . that I must be exaggerating. Oh, I could tell just what he was thinking while he sat there on his fat behind in that plushy office that we taxpayers support. He·thinks I'm an hysterical old female with a persecution complex. But how does he explain the fact that the dog died in convulsions after eating the food that had been poisoned for my special benefit? How do you think he explains that?"

Shayne said politely, "I have no idea. I do know Will Gentry quite well, and he's an efficient and honest police officer."

"But none of them will listen to me," she said grimly. "They all listen to that simpering hussy who married John for his money, and to her paramour who signed the death certificate."

"For the dog?" asked Shayne with interest.

"Of course not for the dog. For John. That young whippersnapper *she* brought in and foisted on my brother after old Dr. Jenson died two months ago. I

9

warned John against him, but he wouldn't listen to me. Oh, no! The only person he listened to was Anita."

"The death certificate?" said Shayne patiently. "Did it specifically state a heart attack?"

"Naturally. What else would you expect a widow's lover to say about her husband's death? Would you expect *him* to suggest an autopsy . . . knowing full well it must be poison?"

"Let's get back to the dog," said Shayne patiently. "When did it die . . . and how did it come to eat your food?"

"Because I fed it to him out of my plate, that's why." Henrietta Rogell's voice was grimly triumphant. "At supper last night. After I had spoken my mind to them plainly, and I could see they were frightened. I told them right out that I knew John had been poisoned by one or all of them, and I intended to prove it. I warned them I was going to force an autopsy on John before he was cremated tomorrow, and I could see they were frightened. So I had this premonition when the buffet supper was served. It was such a perfect opportunity to get rid of me that I was suspicious. And when I tasted my creamed chicken I *knew*. And I slipped some on a saucer to her nasty little dog and he lapped it up. And ten minutes later he was dead. And your efficient and honest chief of police says *that's* no proof," she went on bitterly. "Just a coincidence, he says . . . or an accident. And he says his hands are tied because the chicken was all thrown down the garbage disposal and there's nothing left to analyze. Why not the dog? I asked him. And I ask you. Wouldn't *that* be proof that they tried to kill me? But dear little Daffy is already buried and can't be disturbed. Why not? Because he was the darling of Anita's heart and she just can't bear to think of his sacred remains being desecrated by some bad old doctor making a stomach analysis. And your Will Gentry says he can't legally do a thing if she refuses permission to dig him up."

When she stopped long enough to catch her breath, Shayne said mildly, "Let's go back to supper last night and exactly what happened. You spoke of *them* several times . . . saying you warned them you were planning to have an autopsy on your brother before his body is cremated. Exactly who is 'them'?"

"Anita and that no-good brother of hers, and Harold Peabody and Dr. Evans," she said promptly. "I'm sure they're all in it together. That is, I think Harold planned it all and put her up to it . . . and then with Dr. Evans twisted around her little finger the way he is, it was in the cards for him to cover up for her. And I wouldn't be surprised if that chauffeur and Mrs. Blair were mixed up in it too," she added darkly. "The way I've seen Anita looking at the chauffeur and rubbing against him when she thought nobody was looking. And even Mrs. Blair is changed since John married Anita. I always thought that she and John . . . well."

She shook her head and shrugged and continued briskly, "So I made sure all of them were there when I told them right out that the wool wasn't pulled over my eyes. Those four sitting there guzzling John's liquor with his funeral tomorrow, and Mrs. Blair coming in and out from the kitchen fixing the table, and Charles lolling out in the kitchen listening to every word that was said. Any one of those six could have slipped the poison into my little chafing dish of creamed chicken because they were all having a casserole of curried shrimp and I'm allergic to seafood and every one of them knew the creamed chicken was just for me and no

11

one else would touch it. So it was safe enough, and I wouldn't be here to tell you about it if I hadn't thought to try it out on her dog first."

"And you say all the rest of the special dish prepared for you was disposed of after the dog died?" Shayne asked with interest.

"You can be sure of that. By the time I called the police, and the detectives got there . . . not a smidgen of chicken left. Not even the pot it was cooked in. All washed clean as a whistle. And the dog already taken out by Charles to be buried so the detectives couldn't even look at it. And *still* your chief of police can't see anything suspicious in all that. And if something isn't done by this time tomorrow before the funeral, it'll be just too late. Because John will be burned up and there'll never be any proof he was poisoned by the woman he married and the men she's been carrying on with right under his nose in his own house."

"Will Gentry," said Shayne thoughtfully, "is hedged in by a lot of official rules and regulations. Even though he was personally suspicious, there's hardly any official action he could take."

"But you're not," she said tensely.

"I'm not hedged in by anything except my own conscience," he conceded with a wry grin.

"Chief Gentry intimated as much . . . when he advised me to consult a private detective if I wasn't satisfied with the official investigation made by his men."

"Gentry sent you to me?" Shayne asked in surprise.

"Not in so many words. I did ask him to recommend a private detective and he refused. But I've read about some of your cases, of course, in the papers, and when I asked him point-blank whether even half of the things they say about you are true, he laughed and said just about half. But I got the impression he would be personally pleased if I did come here."

"We have worked together in the past," Shayne agreed. He leaned forward to mash out the very short butt of his cigarette in a tray, and asked abruptly, "Exactly what do you want me to do, Miss Rogell?"

"Why . . . it seems obvious to me. Have the dog's body dissected and analyzed at once. Even Chief Gentry agreed with me that if it were proved my creamed chicken was poisoned he would feel that was sufficient evidence for ordering an autopsy on John."

"You say the dog is already buried?"

"Oh, yes. Anita saw to that. She had Charles remove it at once and take it out to bury it on the grounds. Last night while the detectives were there, they asked Charles where the grave was, and he refused to tell them after Anita ordered him not to. I really think the detectives would have dug it up for examination if they'd known where to find it, but I guess they felt they had no authority to force him to tell them."

"Neither have I," said Shayne bluntly. "Without the dog's body, I don't see what I can do."

"Find it," she shot at him grimly.

Shayne shrugged. "It may be difficult . . . particularly if the chauffeur is as intimate with Mrs. Rogell as you imply."

"Take my word for it, he is," she told him sharply. "But you call yourself a detective and I assume you plan to charge me an outlandish price for your services . . . so I suggest you start detecting. Finding the day-old grave of a little dog on the grounds of our estate should not be a superhuman task."

Shayne grinned at her suddenly and rumpled his red hair. There was something damned likable about the old girl and her unshakable convictions. He said cheerfully, "All right. I'll start detecting. But there's the small matter of a retainer first."

"How small a matter?" she demanded, gimlet-eyed.

"Say five hundred. You can leave a check with my secretary on your way out."

"Isn't that somewhat . . . excessive?"

He met her gaze coldly. "It all depends on your point of view, Miss Rogell. As I explained before, my secretary will be happy to furnish you with a list of investigators who will charge between thirty and fifty dollars a day."

Her clear, blue gaze locked with his for a number of seconds. Then she arose composedly and said, "I will be happy to leave a check with your secretary."

Shayne arose with her. "One final thing," he said as she neared the door. "If you're serious in believing someone at the Rogell house tried to poison you yesterday, I'd move out of the house fast."

She turned with her hand on the knob and smiled for the first time since she had entered his office. It was a wintry smile, but a smile none the less. "I am not a complete fool, Mr. Shayne. I took that elementary precaution last night. For the time being, I am occupying a suite at the Waldorf Towers. Where I shall remain until I can return to the house I have lived in for thirty years without fear for my life." She opened the door and went out with a queer sort of dignity in her mannish stride.

Shayne frowned and went thoughtfully to the water cooler where he withdrew two paper cups and nested them inside each other. Then he opened the second drawer of a steel filing cabinet and lifted out a bottle of cognac, wrestled the cork out with his teeth and poured a moderate portion of amber fluid into the inner cup.

Lucy Hamilton came through the door with flushed

14

cheeks as he returned to his desk and took a tentative, pleasurable sip of cognac.

"I took notes over the inter-com, Michael. Why did you insist that she give you such a large retainer? Do you realize it practically broke her heart to write that check? I don't see how you think you're going to find a dog's grave on the Rogell estate. Do you realize it's a huge place? Ten or fifteen acres along Brickel Boulevard?"

Shayne said equably, "Five hundred bucks was one way of finding out whether she really believes all the stuff she told me. Get Will Gentry on the phone, angel, and I've got a strange hunch you're going to be the one who finds the dog."

"Me? Michael Shayne! If you think I'm going to go out . . ."

He cut off her indignant response with a negligent wave of his hand. "Let me talk to Will first."

Chapter two

When the chief's heavy voice rumbled over the wire, Shayne said pleasantly, "Hi, Will. How big a cut do you expect out of my fee from Miss Rogell?"

Will Gentry chuckled. "So the old girl came to you, did she?"

"After our tax-paid police force turned her down. What *is* the dope . . . confidentially?"

"Are you actually taking her case?"

"I've got her check for five C's as a retainer," Shayne told him equably.

"Did she bleed while she wrote it?"

"I gather she does hate to part with money," said Shayne cautiously. "But, damn it, Will, I sort of like the old biddy. Give me the dope on her brother's death."

"There just isn't anything to go on, Mike. We checked it out from A to Z. John Rogell was sixty-eight years old and has had a serious heart condition for years. Been under the care of Dr. Caleb Jenson for many years until the doc kicked off himself a couple months ago. Since then, a Dr. Albert Evans has been seeing the old boy twice a week. Evans has a good reputation, and he signed the death certificate without the slightest hesitation."

"Henrietta says she's in love with him."

"Plus everything else wearing pants that ever came to the house," snorted Gentry. "Hells bells, Mike! If Anita Rogell were servicing every man Henrietta accuses her of, the woman would have to be a nympho to end all nymphos."

"Is she?" asked Shayne equably.

"I haven't met the girl." Gentry paused, and went on more seriously, "Donovan and Petrie covered the whole deal. They do say the girl is put together right and has what looks like hot lips and a roving smile. But, hell! She's in her early twenties and Rogell was sixty-eight, so what can you expect?"

"That she might be eager to be rid of him so she could take on a younger man like Dr. Evans," said Shayne promptly.

"Sure, there's that. Or the chauffeur or even Harold Peabody who are both on Henrietta's list. But I tell you, Mike, we checked every angle. I had Doc Higgins go over the complete record of the Rogell case in Jenson's files. And Jenson's secretary told him privately that Jenson had urged Rogell not to marry . . . had predicted that just this would happen if he took on a twenty-three-year-old sex-pot like Anita."

"You mean Jenson warned him his heart wouldn't stand it."

"Exactly."

"Then maybe Anita did kill him," said Shayne thoughtfully. "If she knew how serious his condition was and kept egging him on beyond his physical ability."

"Maybe she did," agreed Gentry. "It wouldn't surprise me one damned bit. But that's not a crime, Mike. Not according to the statutes, it isn't."

"All right, I understand why you passed up Henrietta's accusations after John's death. But what about

17

last night? The little dog that died after he ate her creamed chicken. That looks pretty clear-cut to me."

"Sure it does, hearing Henrietta tell it. But the dog had been pretty sick a couple days ago. Did she tell you that? In fact, it was one of those inbred, pampered little bitches that was always having stomach upsets."

"But it never died of convulsions before, ten minutes after eating a plate of creamed chicken."

"No, it never did," agreed Gentry promptly. "And I'd run a test fast enough if I had the body. But I haven't. It was already buried by the time Donovan and Petrie got to the house."

"A suspicious circumstance in itself," Shayne pointed out. "Why the unseemly hurry?"

"Sure, it's suspicious. On the other hand, there was Anita having hysterics all over the place because of her little pet's death, and her almost pathological horror of any sort of corpse. That's why she urged her husband to put a clause in his will that he should be cremated, and why she hysterically ordered the chauffeur to bury Daffy within minutes after her death."

"So it was Anita who urged Rogell to put a cremation clause in his will?"

"She doesn't deny it. She has a similar clause in her own will."

"I still think the dog should be dug up and analyzed."

"So do I," agreed Gentry promptly. "Give me proof that the creamed chicken killed her and I'll get an autopsy on Rogell."

"It still seems like a police job to me, Will. You've got the authority to demand that the dog be produced."

Chief Gentry sighed strongly and said, "Listen, Mike. John Rogell was a multimillionaire and a very important citizen in Miami. His widow is now a multimillionaire

18

and a very important citizen. Just to put it very bluntly, they pay a lot more taxes than Miss Henrietta Rogell."

"I never knew taxpayers were so important to you."

"They pay my salary, meager though it is," said Gentry. "As Henrietta scathingly pointed out to me this morning." He paused and then burst out angrily, "Why in hell don't you get to work and earn your retainer?"

Shayne said, "All right. I will," and hung up.

He sat for a moment, tugging thoughtfully at his left ear lobe, and then opened a drawer of his desk to lift out a Classified Telephone Directory. He settled back and turned the pages slowly, wondering what alphabetical listing to look under. After a couple of false attempts, he found the listing he wanted and made a notation of the address. Then he got up briskly and went to the outer office where he lifted down his panama from a rack near the door and glanced at his watch.

"I have to go out for an hour or so," he told Lucy at her desk behind the low railing. "Grab some lunch while I'm gone and be back by one-thirty or two. I expect to have a very important assignment for you."

"Now, if you expect me to go out digging up dead dogs, Michael Shayne . . ." she began stormily, but he interrupted her with a briskly reproving, "You know I wouldn't ask you to do anything like that, angel."

He started out the door, paused and turned back. "Have you got the morning *Herald?*"

"Right here." She lifted a newspaper from in front of her. "I've been reading the item about the curious death of Mrs. Anita Rogell's very highly bred and very expensive Pekinese last night. Her registered name was Somber Daffodil Third, but her mistress always called her Daffy."

"So it's actually written up in the paper," said Shayne,

openly pleased. "Anything about suspicion of poison?"

"Not a word. I guess they wouldn't dare . . . it being John Rogell's widow."

Shayne nodded and said, "I guess not." He strode out and was absent for a little more than two hours. Lucy was typing a letter when he returned, and he paused at the railing to ask, "Had your lunch?"

She nodded and he said, "Come in my office a moment."

When Lucy entered, he seated her firmly in the client's chair beside his desk and drew a beautifully printed, four-color, four-page brochure from his pocket. He placed it in front of Lucy and leaned over her shoulder to look down at it admiringly.

The cover was done in soft pastel colors. It showed a beautiful blue Persian cat on one side, facing a proud, black French poodle on the other. Between the two animals was an archway of weathered gray stone with an orange sunburst glowing through it from a distance. Neatly lettered on the archway were the words: *Pet Haven Eternal.*

Lucy looked at it wonderingly, caught her lower lip between her teeth and glanced up at him. "What on earth, Michael?"

"Look inside," he told her gleefully. "Just *read* what Haven Eternal offers bereaved pet-owners. You'll never believe it if you don't. Private burial plots, individually landscaped. Artistic grottos with sculptured friezes, and with iridescent colored lights that glow automatically from dusk till dawn . . . at a slight extra charge. A private chapel with piped-in organ music. A crematorium for those who wish that method of disposal. Rosewood caskets in all sizes, lined with varicolored satins. Read it for yourself," he urged, turning to the first page. "Every word of it. You'll never believe it otherwise."

20

He swung away to the water cooler and poured himself a drink while Lucy Hamilton sat at the desk bemused, reading the printed words describing *Miami's Most Beautiful and Most Exclusive Pet Cemetery*.

When she turned the last page she looked up at him, shaking her brown curls vigorously. "But this is utterly fantastic, Michael. Do people actually *go* for this? It's morbid and unhealthy. It . . . it makes me sort of sick to my stomach."

"But you're not one of the Anita Rogells of this world," Shayne told her easily. "Don't you think she might find this brochure completely fascinating?"

"Well . . . from what Henrietta said about her . . ." Lucy paused uneasily, studying Shayne's bland expression. "You mean you think she might be persuaded to have her beloved Daffy disinterred and moved to this repulsive place?"

Shayne shrugged and said, "Seems reasonable. And I think you're the one to persuade her."

"Me? Now see here, Michael . . ."

"All in the interest of justice," he told her soothingly. "If her Peke wasn't poisoned, what's the harm? The little darling ends up at Haven Eternal in much nicer surroundings than she has at present. She can even be cremated if Anita wants that . . . *after* her stomach contents have been analyzed. Sure, you can do it, angel. You look the part okay. Just memorize a few of the salient points in that brochure, and work out a sales pitch. Notice the place on page three where it says they are so discreet that a private car will call if desired, and an attendant in plain business suit will see to removing the remains of the departed pet. That's me," he explained with a grin. "I'll turn up with a shovel as soon as you phone me that it's all set. Here, I got this made for you," he went on persuasively, opening his wallet and extracting a freshly printed business card. In large Gothic type, it said *Pet Haven Eternal,* and in small type in the lower left hand corner it said: *Miss Lucy Hamilton.*

"This should get you in to see the grieving widow," he told her briskly. "From then on it should be duck soup for a gal of your talents. You'll note the brochure very discreetly doesn't even mention any prices, so you're on your own if the matter of cost seems a major consideration. I know she's probably heir to several millions, but sometimes these people squeeze a buck tighter than you or I do. So make the terms as attractive as you want. After it's all over we'll actually take Daffy to Haven Eternal and get her put away in style. What's anybody got to lose . . . except the poisoner?" He added grimly, "If Daffy was poisoned."

Lucy Hamilton shook her head, fluffing out her hair angrily. "Michael Shayne! You're the darndest guy. Why I keep on working for you . . ."

He laughed at her. "Because you love it. You know you wouldn't pass up this opportunity for anything. Take fifteen minutes to study up on the subject," he said generously. "And when you get out there keep your eyes open and your wits about you. See the housekeeper if you can, and Anita's brother who's living off her. And the chauffeur . . . especially in relation to Anita. I'm depending on you, angel," he went on seriously. "We've got to earn that five hundred bucks we extracted from Henrietta. Don't forget you're the one who insisted we needed a client and made me finish my drink and fixed me up pretty so she wouldn't be revolted when she saw me. That makes it your responsibility. And it's got to be done this afternoon. John Rogell is due to be cremated tomorrow unless we get evidence enough to order an autopsy on him."

"But how will I ever explain that I know about Daffy?"

"That item in the paper," Shayne reminded her. "It's a perfect excuse. Hell, if the Haven Eternal people were on their toes they'd already have contacted her. Let's hope they haven't."

Chapter three

A long curving macadamized drive led off Brickel Avenue through beautifully landscaped grounds to the turreted mansion that John Rogell had built on the bay front more than thirty years before. It was constructed of rough slabs of native limestone, aged and weathered by the years and the tropical sun. A rakish two-toned convertible and a sleek, black Thunderbird were parked under the long porte-cochère, and Lucy Hamilton pulled her light sedan up behind them.

She had stopped by her apartment to put on a wide and floppy-brimmed white hat, and she wore spotless white string gloves on the hands gripping the steering wheel nervously. In the neat white leather handbag on the seat beside her reposed the brochure from Haven Eternal, and the printed card her employer had given her was in a cardcase beside the brochure.

She sat motionless behind the wheel for a moment after shutting off the motor. There was a bright sun overhead, but the front of the house was shaded by huge cypress trees, and a light breeze from Biscayne Bay swept around the corner of the house behind her.

She drew in a deep breath with palpable effort, slowly expelled it, then unlatched the door at her left and picked up her bag. She circled between her car and the rear of the Thunderbird to wide and worn stone

24

steps leading up to a white-columned veranda running the full length of the front of the house. She crossed weathered boards to the double oak doors and put the tip of her forefinger firmly on the electric button.

Nothing happened for what seemed to her a long interval, and her courage slowly ebbed away while she waited. During the years she had been Michael Shayne's secretary and only employee, she had successfully carried out many difficult and some dangerous assignments to help him on his cases, but this one today, she felt, was the most weird and bizarre she had ever attempted.

She was in such a state of bemusement that she could not repress an open start of nervousness when the right-hand door swung open silently.

A sullen-faced maid stood on the threshold of a long, dim hallway facing her. The girl wore a neat, black uniform with white lace at the wrists and neck, and she had pouting lips and wary eyes.

She said, "What is it, ma'am?" in a singsong voice that contrived to convey a faint impression of insolence.

Lucy said, "I'd like a moment with Mrs. Rogell."

The maid tightened her lips momentarily and said, "Madame is not at home to anyone."

Lucy smiled pleasantly and said, "I think she'll see me," with a lot more assurance than she felt. She unsnapped her bag and took out the cardcase, extracted the square of white cardboard and offered it to the maid. "Please take her my card."

The girl pressed her hands against her sides and said primly, "I couldn't disturb Madame while she's resting."

Lucy Hamilton lifted her chin arrogantly and said, "I didn't come here to argue with servants. Take my card to Mrs. Rogell at once." She took a step forward as she spoke, thrusting the card into the girl's face so her hand lifted instinctively to take it.

She backed away, saying sullenly, "You wait here and I'll see."

Lucy said, "I have no intention of waiting on the doorstep," and moved into the hall, closing her bag and pressing it to her side under her right elbow.

The maid gave way reluctantly, closing the door and moving aside to an archway with drawn portières, drawing them aside ungraciously and muttering, "You can wait in here then, if you insist."

Lucy went into a large, square, somber room lined with dark walnut bookshelves laden with books in dark leather bindings. There were massive leather chairs in the room, and a man stood in the far corner with his back turned to her. He was bent over a portable bar, and Lucy heard the clink of a swizzle-stick against glass. He wore light tan slacks and a red and yellow plaid sport jacket, and when he swung about to face Lucy with a highball glass in his hand she saw he was a fair-haired young man of about thirty with a wispy mustache and suspiciously high color in his cheeks for a man of his age.

He smiled quickly, showing slightly protruding upper teeth, and exclaimed, "By Jove, there. You've arrived just in the nick of time to save me from a fate worse than death. Drinking alone, you know? And long before the sun has swung over the yardarm." His voice was thin and a trifle high, but he exuded friendliness like a stray mongrel who has just received his first kind word in weeks.

He advanced toward Lucy, his smile becoming a beaming welcome. "Whatever you're selling, I'll take a lot of. Provided, of course, that you have a drink with me first. My name's Marvin Dale, you know. How long has it been since anyone has told you how gorgeous you are?"

Lucy couldn't refrain from smiling. "I'm Lucy Hamilton to see Mrs. Rogell. It's a little early for a drink, and I have nothing at all you'd want to buy."

"Let me be the judge of that." He stood close to her and she saw that his eyes were greenish-blue and had a ferrety gleam in them as they traveled down audaciously from her face over trim bosom and neat waist, hovered approvingly over nicely rounded hips and then moved downward to well-fleshed calves and slender ankles.

"Ve-ry nice. Every bit of it if you'll allow me a snap judgment with so many clothes intervening." He took hold of her left elbow and firmly led her toward the bar. "Of course it's a little early for a drink, but never too early. Wasn't it Dorothy Parker who said, 'Candy is dandy; but liquor is quicker'?"

"I think it was." Lucy struggled with a desire to giggle. This must be the ne'er-do-well brother Henrietta had mentioned so disparagingly, and Michael had told her to keep her eyes open and learn as much about the different members of the family as she could. Marvin, she realized, was already slightly drunk as well as being more than slightly amorous, and she decided to indulge him to the extent of one small drink.

"If you could make me a gin and tonic," she agreed hesitantly. "A very light one. I have a business matter to discuss with your sister," she added as stiffly as she could.

Marvin released her elbow and beamed at her as he whisked a gin bottle from a shelf beneath the bar, and opened an ice bucket to deposit two cubes in a tall glass. He uncorked the bottle and started to tip it over the rim of the glass, but Lucy took it away from him firmly, saying, "I mentioned a light one, remember? Very light."

She picked up a jigger and poured it less than full, while he remonstrated, "So many people do without really meaning it, you know. Say they want a light one,

27

I mean. I always feel the hospitable thing is to . . ."

"Ply your women with liquor," Lucy carried on for him pleasantly. "But I'm not Dorothy Parker. Tonic, please." She held the glass out and he reluctantly filled it to the brim with fizzing liquid.

"I can see you're not. If you're holding back on the intake, however, because you hope to discuss business with my dear sister today, you may as well relax and have a decent slug."

"I'll settle for this one," Lucy told him, retreating to the depths of a leather-upholstered chair. "I know Mr. Rogell's funeral is tomorrow and I don't like to intrude on her grief, but I did hope to have a moment of her time today."

"Oh, it isn't dear John she's grieving about," Marvin told her with a tight, unpleasant smile. "We've all been expecting that for months. It's her darling Daffy."

"Her Pekinese?" queried Lucy. "Somber Daffodil Third."

"Somber Daffodil Third," he agreed, taking a gulp of his drink and slouching into another leather chair near Lucy's with both long legs draped over one arm of it. "Why not try this position?" he demanded suddenly with something very close to a leer. "It's the only comfortable way to sit in one of these chairs."

"And not very ladylike," said Lucy primly, taking a sip of her mild drink.

"Who asked you to be ladylike?" His leer became more pronounced. "You know what the male cricket said to the female grasshopper?"

"No," said Lucy. "I don't know and I'm not interested."

"Well, he said . . . Oh, I say," Marvin interrupted himself as the maid entered through the portières, "do you have to intrude just now, Maybelle? Miss Hamilton

28

and I are just getting cozy over a drink and I was about to tell her a very funny story."

Lucy got to her feet quickly and set the glass down as she faced the girl questioningly.

Maybelle made the pretense of a curtsy and said, "Madame will see you in her upstairs sitting room, ma'am."

Lucy followed her out quickly without looking back at Marvin.

The maid led her down the vaulted hallway to a wide stairway curving upward to the right, and up the stairs to another wide hallway where she knocked lightly on a closed door before opening it and announcing, "Miss Hamilton."

The boudoir was chintzy and feminine, and the temperature was like that of a hothouse devoted to the propagation of tropical flowers in contrast to the pleasant coolness of the rest of the big, stone house.

And the girl-woman facing Lucy, propped up against fluffy, silken pillows on a chaise-longue was not unlike a rare orchid. There was a look of cultivated fragility, of almost ethereal beauty, in the delicate, finely drawn features of Anita Rogell. Her violet eyes appeared enormous and had a look of haunting melancholy about them which, Lucy realized on closer inspection, had been artfully attained by the skillful use of purple eyeshadow combined with a dusting of gold powder on carefully shaped brows. Her hair, tightly drawn back from cameo-like features, was the exact color and texture of cornsilk with the morning sun glinting on it, and it displayed a wide forehead and tiny, shell-like ears that lay flat against her head.

Only the mouth was a discordant note in the carefully wrought perfection of Anita Rogell's face, and the shock effect of that feature, Lucy knew immediately, had been

29

carefully and unerringly calculated as a vivid contrast with the overall effect.

It was a large, coarse mouth with full, pouting under-lip daringly accentuated with heavy lipstick that had a violent orange tinge. It was hard to describe the effect that garish mouth had against the background of cold fragility that was the dominant characteristic of Anita's face. It was a bold and shameless promise of fire and lust that lay beneath the otherwise placid exterior, a flagrant and provocative flaunting of sexual precocity which would have remained otherwise concealed.

At least, that's the way it struck Lucy as she stepped into the overheated room. She had no way of knowing how it would appear to a man who looked at Anita for the first time, and the fleeting thought crossed her mind that she would give a great deal to get Michael Shayne's reaction to the woman in front of her.

But she said composedly, "I apologize for intruding like this, Mrs. Rogell, but when we at Haven Eternal learned of your bereavement we felt morally obligated to bring to your attention certain of our unique services which have lessened the pangs of grief of other pet-owners and which we sincerely hope will partially assuage your own."

It was a speech she had learned by rote, and she delivered it glibly and with what she hoped was a commendable show of sincerity.

Anita had her card between the thumb and tapering forefinger of her left hand. She glanced down at it with a tiny frown puckering her smooth forehead as Lucy spoke her lines, and said, "I don't think I understand exactly what you want from me."

Her voice was unexpectedly husky and deep, with a rich resonance that seemed to vibrate in the silence after she finished speaking.

"It isn't what we want from you, Mrs. Rogell," Lucy told her. "It's what we feel we can do for you that counts with us. Is it possible that you haven't heard of Pet Haven Eternal?" She made it sound as though such abysmal ignorance on the part of Anita was utterly unthinkable, and the woman nibbled at the bait by saying, "The name does sound familiar, but I really don't know . . ."

"This little booklet will explain much better than I can if I talked for hours," Lucy interrupted her, opening her bag and extracting the brochure. "It will only take a moment of your time to glance through it and determine which of our services you feel would be most suitable to assure your dear Somber Daffodil Third that final peace and utter tranquillity that every owner of a four-footed friend who was so devoted in life must desire for the canine soul that has passed onward over the Great Divide to enter the realm of peace that passeth understanding."

Lucy noticed a peculiarly wary, almost frightened glint in Anita's eyes as she completed this remarkable speech and pressed the booklet into the woman's somewhat reluctant hands, and she thought, "Oh, dear. Did I overdo it that time? I don't think this gal is as dumb as I anticipated. Watch your step, Lucy Hamilton, and get down off your cloud."

Aloud, she said, "By merely glancing through this you will see that we have one of the finest plants in the United States. And I assure you our charges are extremely moderate. We are incorporated as a nonprofit organization and our greatest desire is to be of real help to all those who have suffered the inconsolable loss of a devoted pet."

Anita glanced at the pastel-colored cover and arched her golden eyebrows slightly. "A pet cemetery? I've heard they are quite the vogue around New York, but didn't realize there was one in Miami."

"We all felt you must be unaware of our existence when we read the newspaper item this morning concerning the departure of your Daffy. We don't ordinarily solicit business, Mrs. Rogell, but we did feel it our duty to offer you an opportunity to avail yourself of our help and our trained personnel."

"Do sit down while I glance through this," said Anita absently. "Even though it's too late now to help my Daffy." She paused on the second page. "Really? A crematorium just for pets? Such a wonderful idea! If I had realized all this . . ."

"It's never too late, Mrs. Rogell. We can arrange any service you desire with the utmost promptness. After all, it was just last evening, I believe . . . ?" She paused delicately, and Anita nodded without looking up, turning to the next page with pictures and descriptions of individually designed grottos for those who could afford the tariff.

"Yes. It was just last night. Very suddenly and unexpectedly. But I have a thing about death in any form, Miss Hamilton. An inner horror. A sort of instinctive repulsion that is practically a complex with me." She lifted sorrowful violet eyes to Lucy, closed the booklet and gently tapped it against her knee with a sigh. "I've always felt that purging by fire is the only decent way to dispose of one's mortal remains, and I would so much have liked to have that for Daffy, but I didn't realize it was possible and so I had the little darling buried immediately here on my own grounds overlooking the bay."

"But that was less than twenty-four hours ago," suggested Lucy tactfully. "There's no physical reason . . . that is, if you truly desire cremation there's nothing to prevent it even yet. Our attendants are most discreet and understanding. You can be assured that Daffy will be . . . er . . . disinterred with the utmost loving care and taken directly to our crematorium for the . . . uh . . . final purging by fire which you desire."

"You mean . . . dig her up now?"

"Well, yes." Lucy wanted to add that she didn't believe Daffy would mind one tiny bit, but she bit back the words and went on persuasively. "A single telephone call is all it requires. Within an hour we can have a trained attendant here driving an unmarked car who will attend to all the details with the utmost circumspection." She hesitated a moment and then played what she hoped would prove to be her trump card: "And the cost is so very moderate. You simply won't believe it when I tell you the truly infinitesimal sum that will be required to reduce Daffy to a handful of fire-purged ashes in a Grecian urn of your own choosing . . . or even an individual design hand-crafted by one of our specialists."

She stopped and waited, holding her breath while she calculated swiftly how low a sum she should quote if Mrs. Rogell rose to the bait. She hadn't the faintest idea what the normal charge of Haven Eternal would be for such a deal. Probably in the hundreds of dollars, she guessed. She'd keep it under a hundred, she decided. Ninety-seven-fifty sounded like a nice, enticing figure.

But Anita Rogell shook her head decidedly. "I couldn't do that. I haven't the heart to disturb Daffy now. I'm sure she's comfortable and happy in the spot Charles chose for her final resting place. It would be a desecration to disturb her now."

"I don't see that at all. It's often done . . . you know . . . with human beings. After all, circumstances change . . ."

"No." Anita closed the booklet and held it out to her. "I do appreciate your coming here and all the information you've given me. I'll be sure to mention Haven Eternal to any of my friends who might be interested. But it is too late now to be any help to Daffy."

"Perhaps it isn't, Mrs. Rogell." Lucy Hamilton was thinking fast and extemporizing as she went. "We have a very special service that isn't even mentioned in our regular booklet. It's . . . something we have inaugurated recently for pet-owners who feel they will be happier if their loved ones are buried close to them. You definitely must have a marker for Daffy. A . . . a headboard at least. Something very simple and inexpensive, if you think best. We even have plastic markers today, though we do think that plain granite or marble is more appropriate. And we also do individual landscaping of your own private burial plot," she rushed on, "and provide perpetual care if you wish it. Or you can have one of those cunning grottos built right here on your own grounds over the spot where Daffy is already interred."

Anita shook her head firmly. "Not a grotto, I think. It seems ostentatious somehow. A simple granite stone, perhaps, suitably inscribed, of course . . ."

"Of course," breathed Lucy sympathetically.

"And perhaps the grave could be marked with a border of flowers. . . ."

"With a few carefully selected shrubs discreetly in the background for a perpetual and evergreen reminder that Daffy sleeps there in eternal peace," Lucy went on enthusiastically. "Indeed, Mrs. Rogell, I do feel you are exactly right. It would be a sacrilege to disturb her now, and I know you will be more than happy to feel you have done all that can be done for her."

"How much will that be?" asked Anita Rogell.

34

"We'll have to give you an estimate. Make sketches, you know, and offer you several different plans at various prices. It will run . . . oh, from a minimum of twenty-five dollars up to . . . not more than a hundred I'd say, if you don't wish to be ornate . . . and I can see that you don't. We could get some preliminary sketches and estimates immediately if I could see the spot where Daffy is buried now while I'm here," Lucy suggested matter-of-factly. "As soon as I have the physical layout clearly in my mind, I can start our men to work. It would save the cost of a second trip," she urged.

"Yes. I can see that. But I won't be under any obligation to go on with it until I've seen and approved the plans," said Anita a trifle sharply.

"Indeed not. There is no obligation whatsoever." Lucy laughed flutingly. She stood up. "If you can just give me directions so I can find the grave myself . . . ?"

Anita said, "I haven't inquired directly of Charles myself . . . for the exact spot he chose. I was so overwrought last night that I trusted his taste and good judgment." She dropped a languid hand to an ivory-colored telephone handset beside her and pressed a button before lifting the instrument.

Lucy stood back unobtrusively and watched her closely as she spoke into the mouthpiece. It seemed to Lucy her husky voice had a definable lilt to it and the tight serenity of her features relaxed a trifle as she said, "Charles? Would you please come upstairs?"

She replaced the instrument and said, "My chauffeur will take you to poor Daffy's grave. And I am pleased that you came to talk to me, Miss Hamilton. I think the work you are doing is perfectly wonderful."

"We like to think so, too," Lucy told her. "I find it very . . . rewarding." The final word almost stuck in her throat but she managed to get it out. Suddenly the

35

overheated room and the presence of Mrs. Anita Rogell was almost more than she could stand. "Dear God," she thought to herself, "the things I do in the name of loyalty to Michael Shayne!" But when she had gotten safely away, she knew she would be glad she had come. Because if John Rogell *had* been murdered, and if this sex-mouthed child-bride of his had had a hand in his death, Lucy knew that she would be happy to move heaven and earth to see that justice was done. She didn't know exactly why, but she did know she had never before met a woman whom she detested so swiftly and so heartily. And even as she thought that about Anita, the unbidden question flashed through her mind: *"Would Michael agree with me? How would he react to that almost angelic beauty and that mouth that promises so much? How would any man react to Anita?"*

There was a light rap on the door behind her and she turned to see it open and a stocky young man in dark green uniform with polished leather puttees standing there. He had heavy, cleanshaven features, with piercing black eyes beneath thick brows that met above the bridge of a blunt nose. His chin was square and his lips were full, though somehow they conveyed a hint of cruelty. His manner was informally respectful without being servile, and his voice was a well-modulated baritone as he said, "What is it, ma'am?"

"This is Miss Hamilton, Charles." Anita lifted her left hand toward Lucy. "She is from the Pet Haven Eternal, and I want you to take her out and show her the spot where Daffy is buried. I may decide to beautify the grave."

He looked at Lucy and nodded gravely without speaking, and stepped back into the hall. Lucy went to the door, saying brightly, "Thank you very much for the

time you've given me, Mrs. Rogell. I'm sure you won't
be disappointed."

She stepped gladly out of the hot room into the dimly
cool hall, and followed the chauffeur who stolidly led
her to a narrow rear stairway that led out to the back
of the house.

Chapter four

Michael Shayne was pacing back and forth between the waiting room and his inner office when Lucy Hamilton returned. He swung on her disappointedly and growled, "I've been waiting for a phone call to come and get the mutt. No soap?"

Lucy shook her head, lifting off her floppy hat and stripping off white gloves. "She wouldn't buy it, Michael. She's positive Daffy will be happier buried right there at home."

"You did see her?"

"Oh, I saw her all right. And gave her the pitch. She just didn't fall for it."

"What's she like, Lucy?"

Lucy Hamilton hesitated and took a deep breath before replying, "Like an angel infested with leprosy, Michael." Her eyes were wide and troubled as they met his searching gaze candidly. "How can I say it? She's devastatingly beautiful . . . with a diseased soul."

Shayne said quietly, "You're trying to say you wouldn't put it past her to murder her husband and then try to murder Henrietta, if she decided the old gal was a nuisance."

"I guess that is what I'm trying to say. Yet, I have nothing to go on . . . except for her mouth. And that

38

I'm not going to describe for you. I just hope I'm around the first time you see her."

"Did you manage to see any of the others?"

"A maid named Maybelle who reluctantly let me in. Her charming brother, Marvin . . . and Charles."

Shayne grinned slightly at the change in Lucy's tone when she spoke the chauffeur's name. "Tell me about Charles."

"I got quite well acquainted with Charles in the space of about ten minutes," Lucy said quietly. "He's . . . got something, Michael. It's so darned hard to describe. . . ." Her voice trailed off as she turned toward the gate in the railing that led to her desk. With her profile to Shayne, she went on slowly, choosing her words carefully, "It's a sort of aura about him. Almost a physical emanation. You feel he's completely primitive. Animal-like." She stopped at the railing and turned a flushed face to him.

"All right," she said fiercely. "I'll say it out loud. He makes a woman feel that loving him would be wild and free and wonderful. He makes you feel that he's male and you're female. Without touching me and almost without speaking, he managed to rouse instincts I didn't even know I possessed. I didn't lie with him there in the woods, but . . . for a moment I wanted to. And now . . ." Her voice sank. "I honestly don't know whether I wish I had or not."

After this extraordinary outburst, Lucy dropped into her chair and covered her face with her hands, leaned forward while her shoulders shook violently.

Shayne stood very still and said, "Lucy." When she didn't lift her head, he turned into his office and reappeared in a few minutes with a half-and-half mixture of cognac and ice water in a paper cup. She was still leaned forward over her desk with her face in her hands, shoulders heaving.

His face was somber as he went to her. He put a firm hand on her shoulder and tightened his fingers hurtingly. He said, "Sit up and drink this."

She straightened slowly and took her hands away from tear-streaked cheeks. She looked up at him dully for a moment and then took the cup and obediently emptied it. She crumpled it with a long shuddering sigh and said, "Now I know everything. I'm at least ten years older than Charles, yet he made me feel like a virgin maiden of sixteen."

Shayne said quietly, "He must be quite a guy."

"It isn't anything he *does* or *says*, Michael," she cried out despairingly. "It's the way he *is*. You'll never understand."

"No," said Shayne equably, "I don't suppose I ever will." He lowered one hip to the railing so he was close to Lucy, but he didn't look at her. "You make it sound like a pretty explosive setup, the way you describe the two of them."

"Oh, I suppose I'm exaggerating horribly." He heard Lucy blow her nose, and her voice became more normal. "Good heaven! How melodramatic can you get?"

"What about the brother?"

"Marvin? Oh, he's a weak lush."

Shayne tugged at his ear lobe. "You make it seem more important than ever to get that dog's stomach contents analyzed. Damn it, Lucy! Do you suppose she suspected what you were after?"

"No, I'm sure she didn't." Lucy was composed now, and when Shayne looked at her inquiringly she wrinkled her nose at him and smiled shyly. "I think I've made up my mind," she announced. "I've been arguing with myself all the way back from the Rogell estate. Shall I tell

Michael, or shan't I? I know I shouldn't, darn it. You'll probably end up in a peck of trouble and it'll all be my fault. On the other hand . . ." She paused disconcertingly and opened her leather handbag to rummage inside it.

"Should or shouldn't tell me *what?*" demanded Shayne.

"Where Daffy is buried. If I do tell you, I know perfectly well you'll be out there, as soon as it's dark, digging her up. You'll be trespassing and breaking I don't know how many laws . . . and if Charles should catch you at it . . ." She shuddered and then looked down into her bag with a frown.

Shayne said roughly, "I think I can handle a chauffeur. Do you mean you think *he's* suspicious?"

Lucy drew a folded sheet of paper from her bag and said composedly, "I wouldn't be at all surprised. He didn't say anything, but I could tell from the way he acted. . . ."

"A sort of aura?" suggested Shayne. "Or more like a physical emanation?"

She hesitated with the paper unfolded in her hands. "Don't tease me about it, Michael. I was honestly trying to analyze what happened while I was alone with Charles."

Shayne set his teeth together hard, and a muscle quivered in his right cheek. "All right, angel. Tell me."

"It came to me suddenly when Anita absolutely refused to have Daffy dug up and taken to Haven Eternal. I made up a wild story about us beautifying graves at home and putting up headstones and even providing individual perpetual care if it was desired. And she fell for it. She called Charles in and told him to show me where Daffy was buried, so I could give her an estimate of the cost. So Charles took me down a rear stairway and out the back and along a path leading to the boat-house."

Lucy paused a moment, studying Shayne's face doubt-fully. "It's beautifully landscaped right up to the low bluff overlooking the bay. In back there's a four-car ga-rage with a large apartment above. Charles lives there. The two maids and the housekeeper, Mrs. Blair, have rooms on the third floor of the house," she interpolated. "Charles told me when I asked. And, for no reason at all, he volunteered the information that Mrs. Blair had always had her private suite on the second floor next to Henrietta until Mr. Rogell married Anita. Then she was moved up with the maids."

Lucy paused a moment, eyes downcast. "That might be important . . . in the light of something Henrietta said this morning. I don't know whether you noticed it or not, Michael, but she started to say something about her brother and Mrs. Blair, and then stopped abruptly."

Shayne said, "I remember. So he led you down this path to the boathouse."

Lucy nodded. "And about a hundred feet from the edge of the bluff, where there are wooden stairs leading down to a private dock and boathouse, there's a huge, old cypress tree on the right . . . on the left coming from the boathouse." She unfolded her sheet of paper and studied it for a moment. "I stopped my car as soon as I drove outside, and jotted down some figures. Turn-ing off from the path at right angles to the tree, it's eighteen of my paces to Daffy's grave, before you reach the trunk of the tree, but under the shade. And from the point where you turn off at right angles from the path toward the tree . . . from that point to the top of the stairs is fifty-eight paces. I counted them when I walked down the path pretending I had to get a good view of the bay in order to plan Daffy's landscaping."

Shayne nodded, his face inscrutable. "Is the grave easily distinguishable?"

"It wasn't when he first showed it to me. There's no grass under the tree, and he had smoothed it down so it didn't show very much, but I got him to break off a couple of switches and stick them at each end of the grave so I could find it easily next time I came. I said he might not be around to show me. And that's when I think he started getting a little suspicious. He made a couple of nasty remarks while he was marking it that didn't sound *unsuspicious*."

Shayne nodded and drew a deep breath. "You're terrific, Lucy. If we pull this off and the dog was poisoned, remind me to give you the entire fee we earn from the case as your Christmas bonus this year."

"I've never had a Christmas bonus, Michael."

"Haven't you?" He stared at her. "Why the hell not?"

She laughed softly. "Aren't you going to ask me what happened after he showed me Daffy's grave?"

Shayne said, "No. You'll tell me some day. And, after I've met Charles, I'll be better able to understand why it hit you so hard." He leaned over and lovingly rumpled her brown curls. "I'm sorry I haven't the ability to make you feel like a virginal maid of sixteen, but I'll take some lessons from Charles and maybe . . ."

"Michael!" She blushed and turned her head to press her cheek against the back of his hand for a moment. "It wasn't really as bad as I said. It's just that for a little moment out there alone under the cypress tree with Charles . . ."

Shayne said gruffly, "Forget it. Right now, we've got to find some way of equating your paces with mine." He stood up from the railing and moved back against the wall near the outer door. "You start here," he directed her, "and walk straight through the door into my office to the opposite wall. Count how many steps you take."

Lucy did so, and reported, "Fourteen." Shayne stepped the same distance in his longer strides and made it eleven of his paces.

"Eleven of mine to fourteen of yours," he muttered. "That ought to make some kind of equation. Let's see if I remember my algebra from high school." He got a sheet of paper and wrote down: "11:14 = X:?" He stopped and asked Lucy, "How many of your steps from the top of the stairs to the place where you turned off at right angles to the tree?"

She looked at her paper. "Fifty-eight."

Shayne completed his equation by replacing the questionmark with 58. He studied it for a moment with a frown, and then multiplied 11 times 58. He wrote down: "14X = 638," and then divided 638 by 14 and announced triumphantly, "Forty-five and eight-four-teenths of my paces equal fifty-eight of yours. What was the other distance you paced from the grave to the path?"

"Eighteen. I didn't know you could do algebra, Michael."

"One of my minor accomplishments," he told her with a wave of his big hand. He multiplied 18 by 11 and divided the result by 14 and said with satisfaction, "Just a trifle over fourteen of my steps from the path to the grave. Perfect, Lucy. A licensed surveyor couldn't have done better. How far is the boathouse, approximately, from the garage?"

"It's . . . I don't know. A good little distance. There's a lot of shrubbery between, and the path winds quite a lot."

"Out of earshot?"

"Oh, yes. Michael, do you really think you should . . . ?"

44

He nodded emphatically. "I think I'll try my luck fishing from a rowboat on the bay about dusk tonight. I'll have to manage to locate the Rogell boathouse before dark from out on the bay. That may present a problem." He frowned thoughtfully and glanced at his watch. "Get Tim Rourke on the phone, angel. He's pretty good with a pair of oars."

Lucy compressed her lips and went back to her desk without protesting further. When she had Timothy Rourke on the wire, the redhead said, "Are you very busy, Tim?"

"No more than usual." Alerted by the detective's casual tone, the *Daily News* reporter added, "Not too busy to get on the trail of a story."

"How'd you like to go fishing?"

After a brief silence, Rourke demanded incredulously, "This *is* Mike Shayne, isn't it? Did you say fishing?"

Shayne grinned at the phone and said, "That's right. You know, in a rowboat on the bay. With poles and lines with hooks on them."

"What are we going to fish for, Mike?" asked Rourke resignedly.

"A dead dog."

Rourke said, "I see." There was a longer pause this time, then the reporter demanded hopefully, "Have you got in on the Rogell deal?"

"I just suggested going fishing for a dead dog. You want to go along?"

"You bet. When?"

"I think the best time will be shortly after dark, but we should take a boat from the Fisherman's pier a little before sundown. Can you meet me there about seven?"

Rourke said, "Will do," and Shayne caught him before he could hang up:

"Know where you can get hold of a shovel?"

"What kind of shovel?"

"One that digs . . . in the ground."

"I've got a short-handled spade in the back of my car. Look, Mike. If it is the Rogell thing . . ."

Shayne said blandly, "Bring your short-handled spade along, Tim. Fisherman's Wharf at seven."

Chapter five

At early dusk that evening a small rowboat was quartering lazily about a half mile offshore on the smooth surface of Biscayne Bay some two miles southwesterly from the municipal docks. There were two men in the boat. Michael Shayne sat in the stern, hunched over with elbows on his knees, wearing a newly purchased, cheap straw hat, and with a fishing rod extended over the stern trailing a line in the water with an unbaited hook on the end of it.

Timothy Rourke sat toward the bow facing Shayne's hunched back and rowing easily. He had a bottle of bourbon between his feet, and he shipped his oars at brief intervals to take a sip from the bottle. Rourke was very thin and bony, with almost emaciated features, and he grimaced as he shipped his oars again and looked down at the palms of his hands. "I'm getting blisters, Mike. How about you taking over?"

Shayne said, "Sure. But right now let's drift for a while." He studied the curving palm-lined shoreline through narrowed eyes, and said, "I'd guess one of those three boathouses opposite us must be the Rogell place."

"Seems about right," Rourke agreed. "But which one? We've got to decide that before dark."

Shayne said, "We can row in closer after a little. Lucy

said there was a private dock and stairs leading up the bluff."

"*You* can row in," Rourke said shortly. He shaded his eyes to study the three boathouses with Shayne, and announced, "There's someone down at the center dock. If we could get in close enough to ask him . . ."

"Looks to me like he's getting out a boat. Maybe we can intercept him without being too obvious about it." Shayne turned on his seat to stretch out a long arm. "Let me have a shot of that rotgut before you pass out."

Rourke grinned amiably and passed him the bottle. The little boat rocked gently on the very faint swell, and there was utter silence and tranquillity in the early evening air until it was broken by the rapid put-putting of an outboard motor from the shore.

Shayne took the bottle away from his mouth, making a wry face at the taste of Tim's whisky, and said with satisfaction, "He's headed out in this direction. Get your line over the side and make like you're fishing too. If he's on fishing bent, he'll never be able to resist stopping by to see how we're doing."

Rourke grunted and leaned forward to lift a jointed trolling rod that had been furnished them by the owner of the rented boat. He stuck it over the side and let out line so the weighted hook sank beneath the surface. "Just so he doesn't pull up close enough to see the shovel and wonder what in hell we're doing with it on a fishing trip."

"Toss your trenchcoat over it." The small skiff with its outboard motor pushing it through the water was describing a curving route that would bring it close to the drifting rowboat. They could see there was only one figure in the rear handling the tiller, and as it approached closer they could see it was a lad in his early teens. True to the tradition of fishermen, he did cut his

48

outboard as he swept in to cross their bow, and they saw he was a fresh-faced, deeply tanned youngster with a crew cut and an ingenuous smile as he hailed them with a true-to-form, "Having any luck?"

"Not a damned bite so far," Shayne called back disgustedly. "Are there any fish in this bay, or is that just a Chamber of Commerce come-on for Yankee suckers?"

The lad chuckled delightedly as his skiff drifted past forty feet beyond their bow. "Plenty of fish all right, if you know where to look," he told them, as condescending as only youth can be. "But, heck, it's a mile deep hereabouts. You got to get out to the reef about two miles that-away." He waved his hand in an easterly direction. "I'm going out to anchor if you wanta follow along. Just about good dark is when they start biting."

"Just about good dark we'll be back at the wharf where we belong," Rourke grunted. "Say, are you from the Rogell place?"

"Naw. That's the next one south from us. None of them ever do any fishing." The lad spat in the water to express his contempt for neighbors who didn't fish, and leaned over to pull the starting rope of his motor. It caught at once and he surged on eastward with a wave of his hand for the two landlubbers who thought all you had to do was drop a hook in the water to catch fish.

"Now that," said Shayne feelingly, looking at the wake of the departing skiff, "is what I consider a fine, outstanding example of All-American youth. We've got it made, Tim," he exulted, transferring his gaze to the boathouse indicated by the lad. "See those gray stone turrets above the treetops on the bluff. That's just the way Lucy described the Rogell house. We should be able to see lights there after dark to guide us in."

"Yep," said Rourke. "The shamus's luck still holds. What do we do until it's dark enough to try our luck?"

"I think we start rowing back toward the city . . . just in case anyone has noticed us from shore and starts wondering."

"You start rowing," said Rourke, looking at his inflamed palms again.

"Sure," Shayne agreed cheerfully. He stood up and they gingerly changed seats in the rocking boat, and the redhead put the oars in the water and awkwardly maneuvered the bow around to head back toward the city, and sent it lazily in that direction.

Nightfall came slowly and almost imperceptibly to the bay and the lone rowboat making sluggish way northwestward. Lights began to dot the hazy skyline of Miami in the distance, and, watching to their rear as he rowed, Shayne noted, with satisfaction, that the barely seen turrets of the Rogell mansion also showed dimly lighted windows.

He turned the boat at that point, and said cheerfully, "Here we go in for a landfall, Tim. Keep me headed toward it, huh?"

"Sure. Suppose the chauffeur did get suspicious of Lucy this afternoon and is keeping watch?"

"We'll cross that bridge when we come to it," grunted Shayne, laying his weight into the oars awkwardly but with enough brute strength to send the boat angling shoreward at good speed. "He'll have no reason to expect anyone to come by water, so we'll do all our talking now and go in to the dock as quietly as we can. I'll go up the stairs first, Tim. You follow behind with the shovel while I locate the grave. Forty-five and a half paces up the path from the top of the stairs. Then right-angle to the left off the path toward a big cypress for fourteen steps. There should be a stick at each end of the grave to mark it."

In a subdued voice, Rourke said, "Right. When you get in a little closer you better quit rowing and give me an oar. I can scull us in with half the noise those oarlocks make."

They indulged in no further conversation. There was no moon, but the sky was clear and bright starlight glinted on the surface of the bay. Facing toward Shayne in the stern, Rourke kept his eyes fixed on the third-floor lights of the turreted house and kept the boat roughly on course by lifting one hand or the other. When he judged they were as close to shore as was safe, he held up both hands with his palms upward toward the rower, and leaned forward to take an oar which Shayne lifted from the oarlock. Then kneeling in the bow he used as a guide the small dock and boathouse touched lightly by starlight at the base of the bluff.

When it nosed alongside the dock, Shayne was leaning out the stern with a mooring line to catch a stanchion, and he made it fast with a double half-hitch. He stepped easily onto the wooden dock and moved forward into the shadow of the boathouse where he turned to see Rourke stepping out with the spade in his hand.

There was utter night-silence about him as he climbed the wooden steps in rubber-soled shoes, and his alert ears caught no sound from Rourke behind him.

At the top, he could glimpse a faint blur of light through shrubbery from the big house some distance beyond, and there was enough starlight to outline the path he was to follow. He strode along it, counting his steps carefully, and stopped on forty-five. On his left, fifty or sixty feet away, silhouetted against the sky, was a towering cypress tree. Shayne walked toward it confidently, again counting his paces. At the count of ten, the blaze of a strong flashlight struck him suddenly in the face from a point some twenty feet to his right. He stopped in mid-stride as a resonant voice ordered, "Stand still and put your hands in the air."

Shayne stood still and put his hands in the air. Blinking against the glare of the flashlight, he could see nothing except the glint of metal at the point of origin of the light. The glint of metal moved and the voice said triumphantly, "Keep your hands high in the air. This is a double-barreled shotgun with both triggers cocked. What are you doing on this property?"

Shayne said, "I could say I was waiting for a streetcar, but I doubt if you'd think that was very funny. As a matter of fact I got lost out on the bay in a rowboat in the dark and rowed in to the closest light I could see on shore. I thought I might leave my boat tied up at your dock until daylight tomorrow, and telephone for a taxi to come for me."

Charles's voice had a note of feline ferocity in it as he said flatly, "Nuts. You're that smart private eye, Mike Shayne. I was expecting you after you sent your secretary out to case the layout this afternoon."

"I don't know what you're talking about," Shayne protested. "I'm a tourist from up north and I rented a rowboat . . ."

Behind the unwavering flashlight, Charles spat out an obscene word. "Don't stand there and lie to me. Keep your hands up and turn to your right, back to the path and up to the house. I'll be right behind you and this shotgun is hair-triggered."

Shayne kept his hands high and turned slowly to his right and angled back toward the path. Since leaving the rowboat, he had heard not the semblance of a sound to indicate Timothy Rourke's presence on the scene. He devoutly hoped that Charles had not heard anything either.

52

The light followed him, staying on his face as he passed ten feet in front of a stocky, motionless figure. By narrowing his eyes and looking sideways out of the corners, Shayne was able to minimize the full glare of the light and make out the outline of Charles's figure. The chauffeur held the flashlight in his left hand, with the twin barrels of the shotgun resting across his left wrist following the direction of the light as it followed Shayne. He did not move from his stance until Shayne was well past him, and then the light dipped and wavered, and Shayne heard footsteps stalking his own. He slowed as he reached the pathway leading from boathouse to the garage, but the footsteps also slowed behind him and Charles ordered harshly, "Keep moving toward the house, shamus. There's buckshot in these two barrels."

The voice was not more than ten feet behind him, and the light was steady on the small of his back. Shayne moved on, following the winding path easily by the light of the flash that fell ahead of him on both sides.

The blur of light ahead through the shrubbery grew stronger, and Shayne let his steps drag a trifle, listening intently to see if Charles would unwittingly close the gap between them. It seemed to him that his pursuer moved a couple of feet closer. That would make it eight feet, Shayne calculated, still not close enough to happily come to grips with a shotgun.

But as he approached a thick clump of hibiscus and could discern that the house lights were quite close and bright beyond its shade, he knew it was his last chance to avoid the ignominy of being marched in at the point of a gun like a craven thief. He didn't know how much of his determination was born of the memory of what Lucy had said about Charles that afternoon (what she had left unsaid, actually), but he did know suddenly that he couldn't let the Rogell chauffeur take him like this.

He tensed as he reached the thickest shadow of the hibiscus, braced his heels and flung himself backward and down. As he hit the ground full-length with arms still stretched over his head, there was the terrific blast of both barrels of a twelve-gauge directly over his body.

At the same moment his flailing hands fastened on Charles's ankles and he jerked them from under the man and heard the gun fall to the ground. Then Shayne was on his knees, furiously driving a left and then a right fist into the whitish blur that was Charles's face as he tried to roll away. His left glanced off the chauffeur's cheekbone, but his right connected solidly with mouth and blunt chin at the precise moment the back of the man's head was in contact with the ground.

There was a splendid crunching sound and Charles's head lolled to the side. Otherwise he did not move.

Shayne dragged himself to his feet and exhaled a great shuddering breath, faintly surprised to find that he was still alive. A bright light sprang on at the back of the house beyond the hibiscus, and in the light Shayne stooped to pick up the shotgun by the end of its twin barrels with his left hand. Then he got a firm grip at the back of Charles's neat, green uniform collar, and straightened up and dragged the gun and the unconscious man around the clump of shrubbery into the full glare of a floodlight mounted above the kitchen door and directed across the parking space in front of the garage.

Two women stood just outside the open back door beneath the floodlight looking at him from a distance of forty feet. One was middle-aged and short and somewhat dumpy, Shayne's first glance told him. The other was young and slender and beautiful. She was bare-

54

headed and dressed all in white, and white draperies trailed out behind her as she sped toward him across the parking space, crying out in a choked voice, "Charles? Is that you?"

Shayne got a grin on his face as he stalked forward, dragging Charles and the shotgun behind him. His one fleeting thought was that Lucy was to be deprived of her wish to be on hand the first time he met Anita Rogell.

Chapter six

When she came close, Shayne relaxed his grip on Charles's collar and the chauffeur slumped forward with his face to the macadam. Anita dropped to her knees in front of him and crouched there with her hands on his head and cheek, and cried out tearfully, "Charles! Answer me!"

When Charles didn't answer, she looked up fiercely at Shayne and demanded, "What have you done to him?"

Shayne looked down at the skinned knuckles of his right hand and said, "He'll be all right, Mrs. Rogell. Do you greet all your guests with a double-barreled shotgun?"

Charles moved his head and groaned thickly. Anita bent over him again, crooning softly, and he twisted his body and got the palms of both hands flat on the pavement and hoisted himself up to a half-sitting position. His black eyes were wild and the front of his face was smeared with blood, and the red stuff dribbled off his blunt chin in a slow stream. He spoke groggily through mashed lips and a hole where two front teeth had been, "'S Mike Shayne, Nita. I tol' you. . . ." He choked on a clot of blood and hacked it out of his throat and then slumped down on his side again.

The older woman had reached the scene and Anita got to her feet, ordering her sharply, "Call Dr. Evans at

56

once, Mrs. Blair. Charles is badly hurt. And tell Marvin to come out here if he's sober enough to help. We must get Charles inside."

While the housekeeper scurried away toward the back door, Shayne dropped the shotgun and said, "We don't need any help for that."

He stooped and got his right arm under Charles's thighs, put his left behind the man's lax shoulders and heaved upward with a tremendous effort, lifting the body that weighed fully as much as his own and holding it in his arms with feigned ease while he grinned down into Anita's eyes and asked, "Where do you want him?"

For a moment there was electric silence between them while their eyes locked. Anita trembled slightly and sucked in her upper lip and there was a look in her eyes like a young child contemplating a forbidden delicacy. She said softly, "You're very strong, aren't you?"

Shayne forced himself to swagger forward as though the heavy burden were no effort at all, deriding himself inwardly as he did so with the knowledge that he was acting like a teen-ager flexing his muscles in front of his first love. "Which way?" he ground out through set teeth.

"Here. Through the back door. You'd never get him up to his apartment over the garage." She hurried in front of him, and Shayne followed, his knees almost buckling under the strain, but grimly determined to carry it off.

He was halfway across the parking space and was becoming increasingly aware that he couldn't possibly make it, when Charles fortuitously gurgled something deep in his throat and began making feeble efforts to free himself from Shayne's arms.

The redhead thankfully lowered his right arm to let the chauffeur's dangling feet touch the ground, and got

Charles's left arm around his neck where he levered it down over his own left shoulder. The man was conscious enough to support part of his weight on rubbery legs, and Shayne half carried him on to the back door where Anita was waiting.

"In here." She went through a gleaming modern kitchen to a small room directly off it fitted up as a comfortable sitting room. The housekeeper was talking excitedly into a telephone in one corner, and Shayne thankfully let Charles down on a chintz-covered sofa where he lay very still, glaring up at Shayne balefully.

Mrs. Blair replaced the phone and bustled forward, saying cheerfully, "Dr. Evans will be right here. Now you just lie easy, Charles, and I'll get a cold cloth for that face of yours."

She hurried through the connecting door into the kitchen and Shayne slowly turned his gaze away from Charles's venomous glare to catch a queer look on Anita's face as she stood back and to one side, studying him and not paying the slightest heed to the chauffeur.

It was a melancholy, questing look. At once frightened and somehow exalted. Compounded, Shayne thought, of sheer, lustful desire and passionate hatred. Fragments of Lucy's description of Anita Rogell went fleetingly through Shayne's mind as their eyes locked for a second time within a space of minutes.

Without taking her eyes from him and without change of expression, Anita slowly licked her pointed tongue out over her short upper lip exactly like a cat contentedly licking off cream. Shayne almost thought he heard her purr in the silence.

When she spoke it was not in a purring tone. Her voice was throaty and had a little catch in it. "You're Michael Shayne."

58

He said, "I'm Michael Shayne. Does that give your man license to hunt me down like a mad dog with a shotgun?"

From the sofa, Charles uttered garbled words. Neither of them paid him the slightest heed. They were warily measuring each other like antagonists in a duel to the death.

She sucked in her breath and said, "He warned me you would come tonight. To try and dig Daffy up and take her away."

Beside them and a few feet away, they were conscious that Mrs. Blair had returned from the kitchen and was ministering to Charles with little clucking sounds of sympathy. Neither of them looked in that direction.

Shayne said heatedly, "I don't know what you're talking about. I explained to your chauffeur that I got lost in the dark while fishing, and rowed in to the first shore lights I saw . . . hoping I could call a taxi to take me home. And he met me with a cocked shotgun."

"Why did you send your secretary here this afternoon . . . if not to discover where Daffy is buried so you could come and take her away?"

"My secretary?" said Shayne in feigned astonishment. "Are all of you crazy?"

"She is named Lucy Hamilton, isn't she?"

"That's my secretary's name," Shayne admitted. "As a great many people in Miami know. What of it?"

"Do you deny she came here this afternoon pretending to be from a pet cemetery so she could find where Daffy is buried?"

"Of course, I deny it," said Shayne vehemently. "Why on earth would Lucy do a silly thing like that?"

"Because Charles suspects that John's crazy sister hired you to try and prove Daffy was poisoned by one of

59

us here because she accused us of murdering her brother." Anita spoke the words calmly and simply, as though they were of no consequence at all.

Shayne drew in a deep breath and shook his red head in what he hoped was a gesture of utter bafflement.

"You're way beyond me. I don't follow you at all."

"I did call Haven Eternal after Charles came back from showing Miss Hamilton Daffy's grave and told me he thought she was up to something else. They have no representative named Lucy Hamilton, and they don't even send out people representing them. How do you explain that, Michael Shayne?"

Shayne said, "I don't. Why should I?"

"And then," Anita went on evenly, "Charles remembered reading in the papers that you have a secretary named Lucy Hamilton. You won't deny that?"

"Certainly not," Shayne said heatedly. "This conversation is utterly absurd. Don't you have a drink handy?"

Anita tilted her head and considered him gravely for a moment. Then she put out her hand and Shayne took it in his and she said almost gaily, "Of course there's a drink handy . . . Michael Shayne," and her husky voice made rich music of the name.

With her hand in his, she led him past the sofa where Mrs. Blair was on her knees still, making clucking noises over Charles. They went out of the room and through the kitchen to the wide vaulted hallway that Lucy had described to Shayne, and some thirty feet down the hall toward the front door and through a pair of sliding doors on the right that stood partially open. It was a small conservatory, and the temperature inside was the same as Lucy had described the upstairs boudoir. Still holding Shayne by the hand, she led him to a gleaming refectory table in the center with a white lace cloth on it and a huge silver tray holding a cocktail shaker with a small amount of liquid in it, two long-stemmed cocktail glasses that had been recently drunk from, a bucket of cracked ice, a heavy cut-glass decanter, marked *Crème de menthe* and a quarter full, and another, larger decanter, unmarked, but containing an amber liquor that looked to Shayne's avid eyes very much like long-aged cognac.

She said, "Marvin and I had stingers after dinner. Would you like to mix another batch?"

Shayne squeezed her hand hard and looked down at the top of her shining head which lightly brushed his shoulder. He released her hand and said, "I'd rather have a straight drink." He reached for one of the cocktail glasses and she moved toward a silken bellcord, murmuring, "I'll ring for a clean glass."

Shayne said, "Please don't. I'd much rather use one of these and be alone here with you." He twisted the glass stopper from the large decanter and filled one of the cocktail glasses to the brim. She had moved back close to him when he lifted it to his lips. He breathed in deeply the clean, delightful bouquet from the distillate of sun-ripened grapes, and the tips of her taut, full breasts, behind the silky white of a loose blouse, pressed lightly against his chest as she moved even closer.

She stood rigid, just touching him, her arms straight down at her sides and both hands tightly clenched. Over the rim of his glass, he stared down into her uplifted face. Her eyes were tightly closed and a tear squeezed out of the inner corner of each one and trailed down her lovely, waxen cheeks. Her lips were parted and the tip of her tongue showed between them, and they moved almost imperceptibly, and, faintly as the sound of a muted bell, he heard the whispered words that seemed to well up from deep inside her and not from her vocal cords at all:

"I want you, Michael Shayne."

He set the cocktail glass down without tasting the contents. She stood rigid and unmoving against him. Very carefully, he put his right arm about her shoulders. Her flesh seemed to pulse against his as he put slowly increasing pressure against her shoulders, crushing her against his chest, and her head fell back farther and her lips parted more widely, and then her eyes came open as he lowered his head, and they were unfocused and gleaming, the irises showing enormously large, and when his lips touched hers, her belly and her loins writhed against him and the suction of her mouth on his was avid and compelling.

It was either a brief moment or an eternity that they stood like that, as close as two humans can get. Then Shayne heard the insistent ringing of door chimes from the front, and he slowly released her and stepped back to pick up the cocktail glass in a trembling hand, just as Mrs. Blair hurried past the open doors on her way to answer the front door.

Anita smiled dreamily at him and rested the knuckles of her left hand on top of the table. "I imagine that will be Dr. Evans come to see Charles. He's always so prompt."

Shayne took a gulp of cognac. It burned all the way down his throat to meet but not assuage another sort of burning in the pit of his stomach. He said, "That's nice of Dr. Evans," set his glass down and fumbled a cigarette out of his shirt pocket while Anita sauntered to the gap in the sliding doors and stood there looking out composedly until Mrs. Blair and the doctor hurried by, and said, "Let me know about Charles at once, Doctor. I do hope it isn't serious." She turned back to Shayne and asked serenely, "It isn't, is it?"

"Just a few teeth knocked out, I'm afraid." He looked

down at his raw knuckles and drew in a deep breath. "You were giving me some absurd reason for his attacking me with a shotgun when . . ."

"When you decided you needed a drink," she finished for him. "And it wasn't absurd at all. I'm sure Charles was exactly right and Henrietta did hire you to dig up Daffy and try and prove she was poisoned."

"Was she?" demanded Shayne.

"Poisoned? Of course not. Why would anyone want to do a cruel thing like that? Everyone loved her. Except Henrietta, of course. She hated everyone. If Daffy was poisoned, you can be sure that old bag did it. And maybe she did at that," Anita went on slowly. "It'd be just like her. She could have, you know. Poisoned that chicken herself, and then fed a plate of it to dear Daffy out of spite."

Shayne grinned sardonically. "And then went around and hired a private detective to disinter the dog and prove her guilt? You can't have it both ways, Mrs. Rogell."

"Please call me Anita," she said absently, her forehead furrowed pensively in thought. "Maybe not, but you can be certain no one else in this household would have harmed Daffy."

"How can you be so certain of that?" sneered a rather fruity voice from the hallway, and a fair-haired young man lolled between the parted doors. He swayed a little and clenched a highball glass in his hand, and his bloodshot eyes didn't focus very well. "Nashty-tempered little bitch, I always said. Snapped at my ankle once and, by Jove, you were more worried about me kicking her than about me getting bit. What's all the ruckus about anyhow, sis?" He peered owlishly at Shayne. "Atom bombs going off in our backyard, doctors running hither and yon. You haven't introduced us, you know."

"This is Michael Shayne," said Anita distinctly. "My brother, Marvin."

"The noted private eye, eh?" Marvin blinked at him and moved closer to peer into his face with bleared eyes. "You don't look the part at all, you know. Not like it is on television with all your beautiful blond clients ripping off their clothes and crawling into bed with you first crack out of the box. Does he, sis?" he asked her with a leer. "Can you imagine any beautiful blond clients climbing into bed with this redheaded Mick? I ask you now. You're a blonde and you ought to know. Would you climb in bed with his ugly mug?"

In a coldly vicious voice, Anita said, "Get out of here, Marvin. You're drunk."

"Coursh I'm a little bit drunkie." He smiled vacuously and took one more look at Shayne, shuddered and almost fell over his own feet exiting.

She said, "So much for my brother, Mr. Shayne." A dreamily contemplative expression chased the anger from her face. "I would, you know."

Shayne said, "I know," very matter-of-factly.

She closed her eyes and clasped her arms about her full breasts and shivered. Then she started gliding toward him with her eyes closed.

Shayne emptied his glass and set it on the table and waited for her to reach him.

The voices of Mrs. Blair and Dr. Evans came from the hall, approaching them. Anita stopped three feet from Shayne, unclasped her arms and opened her eyes. The hypnotized expression faded from her face, and she turned and went to the door and asked lightly, "How is Charles, Doctor?"

"As well as can be expected." His enunciation was

64

precise, with a studiedly genteel inflection. "I had to take six stitches and administer a sedative for the pain. Later, he'll have to see a good dentist. I must have the straight of this, Anita. From Charles and Mrs. Blair I am given to understand that some hulking brute of a private detective forced his way onto your property tonight bent on desecrating the grave of your dog, and Charles was injured while defending the place. Have you called the police to lay charges against this ruffian? I am required to report the incident, you know."

"Why don't you discuss it with Mr. Shayne?" Anita moved aside and Dr. Albert Evans stepped through the sliding doors. He was young for a practicing M.D. Not more than his early thirties, Shayne thought. He was slender and of medium height, with slightly protuberant eyes behind gold-rimmed nose glasses attached to a black cord around his neck.

He stopped and looked severely at Shayne, but the detective could have sworn there was the suggestion of a twinkle in his eyes as he asked, "What did you hit Charles with? He insists you attacked him with a large rock."

Shayne held out his right hand with the fist doubled. "If you've any adhesive left you might put a little on my knuckles."

"It's no joking matter," the doctor told him. "It's trespassing, Anita. And assault and battery at the very least. This man should be arrested."

"He claims he lost his way on the bay in a rowboat and put ashore to get help when Charles mistook him for a vandal and threatened him with a shotgun."

"Can you prove that?" demanded Dr. Evans of Shayne.

"Can you prove I didn't?"

"There's still assault with a deadly weapon." The doctor glanced at Shayne's fist and the suggestion of a twinkle was back in his eyes.

"Assault?" snorted Shayne. "While the idiot followed me at six feet with a cocked double-barreled shotgun loaded with buckshot? The slightest misstep on his part would have blown me into two pieces. If anybody lays any charges around here, it'll be me."

"I think Mr. Shayne is right," said Anita sweetly. "Let's be happy no greater damage was done."

"Yes . . . well. . . ." The doctor took off his glasses, blinked rapidly and fiddled with them. "I've done all I can for Charles tonight." He turned to go, but Shayne stopped him.

"If you're going toward town, Doctor, could I bum a ride with you? I meant to call a cab, but haven't gotten around to it yet."

"Why, yes. Certainly, if you like. I go down the Avenue to Flagler."

"Right past my place," Shayne told him genially. He walked past Anita and her fingers swung out to catch his hand as he went by. He pressed her fingertips hard and said, "Thanks for everything, Mrs. Rogell. I hope we meet again."

She dug her fingernails fiercely into the fleshy part of his palm and then released his hand. He followed Dr. Evans down the hall, glancing through portières on the left as he went by and seeing Marvin across the library at the bar intent on mixing himself another drink.

Dr. Evans opened the door and held it for him, and they went across the wooden porch and down stone steps to a neat dark sedan under the porte-cochère.

The doctor put his bag in the back and went around to get under the wheel, and Shayne slid in beside him. He put the car in gear, and as it moved smoothly down the winding drive, he said quietly, "I take it you are a private detective, Mr. Shayne?"

"Yes."

"And I also take it you were attempting to disinter Mrs. Rogell's pet dog to have its stomach contents analyzed?"

Shayne said, "I have no intention of admitting that fact, Doctor."

"Yes . . . well . . ." The sedan turned north on Brickell. "I can only wish you had been successful," the doctor said fretfully. "I confess I'm dreadfully bothered."

"You think the dog was poisoned?"

"I have no opinion in the matter . . . not being a veterinarian. I do wish Mrs. Rogell had not been so precipitate in having the little beast buried. But she has a dreadful complex about death in any form. The result of some childhood trauma, I daresay, though I'm not a psychiatrist either. And the death of her husband, just two days ago, left her dreadfully upset, of course. A remarkable woman, though. She's bearing up exceedingly well."

Shayne said dryly, "Yes. I imagine Anita Rogell will survive okay," with the memory of that tempestuous embrace still rocketing through his body. "I understand you signed the death certificate," he added.

"Certainly I did. I had been attending him for months and was called immediately after his death was discovered."

"Is there any possibility whatsoever, Doctor, that he could have been poisoned?"

"You've been listening to Henrietta," he said bitterly. "Spreading her spleen wherever anyone will listen. Mr. Shayne, if you are an experienced detective, you must know that no competent medical man in his right mind can absolutely rule out the possibility of some kind of poison in *any* death. No matter how normal it may appear on the surface. If we took that fact into consideration, perhaps we should have an autopsy on every cadaver . . . no matter what the circumstances of death."

"Perhaps we should," Shayne said equably.

"Yes . . . well . . ." The doctor slowed as he approached the bridge across the Miami River. "Since that is not accepted practice, I can only tell you there was no scintilla of evidence to give me the slightest doubt that John Rogell's death was the normal and natural result of his heart condition. That is the statement I gave the police, and I stand behind it."

"Right here, Doctor," Shayne said hastily as they drew abreast of his apartment hotel. "Thanks for the lift . . . and for the information." He got out at the curb and lifted a big hand in farewell, waited until the doctor drove on and then trudged across to the side entrance where he climbed one flight of stairs and went to his corner apartment to wait for Timothy Rourke to show up or telephone him.

Chapter seven

It was almost two hours and three drinks later when the door opened and Timothy Rourke shambled inside with his trenchcoat belted tightly about his thin waist, eyes glittering balefully at the tranquil picture Shayne made, sitting at ease in a deep chair with smoke curling up from a cigarette and a drink beside him.

He said, "By God, Mike! You're one who'd come up covered with diamonds if you fell into a sewage pit."

Shayne grinned amiably and asked, "Had rough going?"

"Look at my goddam hands." Rourke strode forward, holding the palms up for Shayne's inspection. They were puffed with blisters, some of which had broken and the red flesh beneath was cracked and bleeding. "Been rowing around in circles on that lousy bay for two hours," grated Rourke, turning aside to a wall liquor cabinet and lifting down a bottle of straight bourbon with the ease of long familiarity. He pulled the cork as he returned to the center table, tilted the bottle over a tumbler containing two half-melted ice cubes and a small quantity of water that Shayne had been using for a chaser. He poured four fingers into the glass, sloshed it about for a moment, and then drank it off in four gulps.

He smacked his lips expressively, draped his knobby

body into a chair across the table and grated, "The things I do for you, Mike Shayne! By God, that dog had better have poison in her belly."

"She has," Shayne said flatly. "You got her, huh?"

"Sure I got her," said Rourke belligerently. "While you were inside getting cozy with the widow. I got a peek through the bushes after the shotgun blasted. I figured I'd take one look at you with your fool head blown off so I could give Lucy the morbid details. And what did I see? You standing there under the floodlight with that unconscious lug in your arms, and that babe fawning up at you like she'd never seen a man before in her life."

"It was a diversionary tactic," said Shayne cheerfully, "to give you an opportunity to do your stuff with the shovel." He reached in his pocket for a small address book and began thumbing through it.

"How was she, Mike? After you got her in the house and dumped the chauffeur?"

"There were too many people around to really find out. Some other time, maybe, I'll give you a detailed report. Where's the dog?"

"Downstairs in my car." Rourke sighed and pulled himself to his feet with a grimace of pain from long unused muscles. He went out to the kitchen to get a fresh glass and more ice cubes for himself while Shayne found the number of Miami's most noted toxicologist, lifted the phone and gave it to the switchboard downstairs.

Shayne spoke into the mouthpiece as Rourke sauntered back and sloshed whisky into the glass: "Is that Bud Tolliver? Mike Shayne, Bud. Can you do a fast job for me tonight?"

He listened a moment and said, "I don't think this will take long. You should be able to handle it right there in your basement lab. Analysis of the stomach contents of a dead dog for poison."

He lifted one eyebrow at Rourke and grinned slightly, holding the receiver inches from his ear as a torrent of protest poured out.

Then he cut in persuasively, "I don't blame you a bit, Bud, but this is a hell of a lot bigger than just a pooch. If I'm right, we're going to get a P.M. ordered on a corpse who's due to be cremated tomorrow. That's why it's got to be fast."

He listened a moment longer and nodded. "I'll bring it right over to your place." He hung up and told Rourke, "Tolliver feels his professional status is being impugned by working on a dog. Coming along, Tim?"

Rourke had sunk back into his chair with tall glass clamped tightly in both hands. He shook his head, got a leather keycase from his pocket and dropped it on the table. "Take my car. It's parked in front with the dog locked in the luggage compartment. Drop Daffy off at Bud's and then come back here, huh? I'm trying to remember something about Henrietta Rogell. If it comes through, I think we can stand a trip to the *News* morgue. If it doesn't, at least I'll be catching up with you." He lifted his glass significantly.

Shayne took the keys and said, "Try to make it come through, Tim."

He went out the door and down on the elevator, through a deserted lobby to Rourke's battered sedan in front.

Bud Tolliver was a bachelor who lived in a five-room stucco house in the northeast section of the city. The porch light was on when Shayne pulled up in front of the house, and the redhead got out and unlocked the luggage compartment and opened it. The tiny body of a Pekinese lay stiff-legged on the floor, its formerly shiny coat matted with dirt, its mouth half open in what appeared to be a derisive grin.

Shayne lifted the light body out by a front and rear paw, carried it up the walk held stiffly out in front of him. The front door opened as he stepped onto the porch, and Tolliver motioned him inside.

The toxicologist was as tall as Shayne, and a few years younger. His head was completely bald, and he had an intelligent, bony face that puckered thoughtfully as he drew aside and looked at the detective's burden. "How long has the pooch been buried?"

"Just about twenty-four hours." Shayne paused inside the neat living room while his host closed the front door and led the way toward the back where he opened a door off the kitchen and switched on a light leading down to his basement laboratory.

Downstairs, Shayne lowered Daffy's remains to a gleaming white enamel table, and brushed off his hands.

"You know I haven't got too much equipment here at home, Mike. Just enough for some simple tests. What am I looking for?"

"She's supposed to have died last evening in convulsions about ten minutes after eating a dish of creamed chicken fed to her by an old lady who suspected it contained poison. On the other hand it's reported that she's been a sickly dog, often subject to stomach upsets."

"The convulsions in ten minutes sound like a solid dose of strychnine," said Tolliver absently, lifting a starched surgeon's garment from a hook on the wall and sliding his arms into the sleeves. "If so, it'll be easy."

"It needs to be definitely tied in with the creamed chicken to give us an open-and-shut case, Bud."

"Sure," the toxicologist said cheerfully, turning to a rack of shining surgical instruments and selecting one. "You want to stick around and watch it done?"

"I don't think so," said Shayne hastily. "Not tonight.

72

Tim Rourke and I have things to do. Call me at home, huh? About how long?"

"Half an hour or so."

Shayne said, "Swell," and went up the stairs quickly while Tolliver bent over the dead dog with professional interest and zeal.

Timothy Rourke got to his feet quickly when Shayne walked into his own apartment ten minutes later. He drained the last of his drink and said triumphantly, "Got it, Mike. Let's run up to the *News* and check it out."

Shayne waited at the door for him to come out, pulled it shut on the latch, and asked, "Got what?" as they went back to the elevator.

"The thing that's been nibbling at my so-called memory ever since you sprung this Rogell deal on me this afternoon. Gives a pretty good sidelight on Henrietta. It was about five years ago, Mike, when she made the headlines with a lawsuit against her brother. Demanding an accounting of his estate and claiming a one-half share for herself. The details are hazy in my mind," he went on as they crossed the lobby. "I forget how it came out. But he made his fortune out west, in mining, I think, and I believe that she claimed she worked in the mines with him and that half his millions were rightfully hers, and she wanted the money legally and in her own name instead of living with him in that big house and having him dole it out to her."

They reached Rourke's car and Shayne asked if he wanted to drive.

The reporter shook his head and opened the right-hand door. "Not with these blisters. Not until I have to."

In the huge file room in the *Daily News* Tower, Rourke led the way confidently down a long aisle lined with filing cabinets, pulling dangling cords to switch on overhead lights as he went. He slowed and finally stopped in front of a cabinet, pulled out a drawer marked Re-Ro.

He fumbled through cardboard folders, drew a thick one out and opened it on a table under a bright light. "Here's the last stuff on Rogell. His obit and so on." He slowly turned clippings over as he spoke, stopped at another batch and looked down with interest at a bridal picture. "And here's the old boy's wedding just a few months ago. The April-December wedding that had the sob-sisters gushing all over the society pages."

Shayne leaned over to study the picture with him. It had been taken on the steps of a local church as the couple left after the ceremony. It was the first picture Shayne remembered seeing of John Rogell. He was tall and lean and leathery faced like his sister, wearing top hat and cutaway. He looked a sound and vigorous sixty in the picture, not like a doddering old man whose heart might be expected to give way under the importunities of a demanding young bride.

Of course, there was a startling difference between the ages of the couple. In her white bridal dress and clutching her wedding bouquet, Anita was radiantly beautiful, the personification of a virginal young bride on the happiest day of her life.

"Mr. and Mrs. John Rogell as they emerged from the noonday solemnizing of their wedding rites," Rourke read dryly from the text beneath the picture. "Hell, if the old boy had three months of that, I'd guess he died happy."

He turned the clippings back slowly. "There were scads of feature stories as soon as news of the engagement broke. It was real Cinderella stuff. It *can* and *does* happen in Miami. Anita Dale. Small-town girl, from a

74

poor upstate family, coming timidly to seek her fortune in the Magic City of sun, sin and sex with a high-school diploma and a six-month secretarial course as her only assets. A filing job at forty bucks a week with the Peabody Brokerage firm . . . and then the jackpot. Like that." He snapped bony fingers and grinned wickedly. "Six months later she sits out in that stone mansion, heir to a lot of millions of bucks. How's that for rags-to-riches in one easy installment?"

"Did you say the Peabody Brokerage firm?"

"Sure. Harold Peabody. She was working there when she met Rogell. Peabody is one of Miami's up-and-coming young financial consultants. Rogell is probably his biggest account, though others have been flocking to him since he got publicity along with one of his secretaries marrying millions. It's pretty well understood he'll be executor of Rogell's estate. But that's all recent history," Rourke added as he flipped back through scattered clippings. "Just routine stuff here. Rogell buys another shipping line, invests a million in an Atlanta real-estate development. Here's what I'm looking for."

He paused at a long front-page story, headlined, SPINSTER SUES MULTIMILLIONAIRE BROTHER.

"This is the day they opened the trial," he muttered. "I covered that first day myself. Let's see . . . if I turn back a few clippings we should find the verdict."

He began doing so, glancing quickly and expertly at a few words or the heading of each story. He stopped after a moment and said, "Here it is," and read: "JURY RETURNS VERDICT IN MILLION-DOLLAR SUIT FOR DEFENDANT."

"She lost it hands down," he told Shayne. "I thought I remembered it that way, but I wasn't sure. The jury felt Henrietta was doing all right as she was . . . sharing the big house with him as his official hostess with charge accounts all over town and a monthly cash allowance a lot bigger than she could possibly spend. All that was brought out in testimony during the trial," he explained. "She never complained that her brother was niggardly or that she actually wanted for anything. Her position was simply that half the money should legally be hers and she wanted it in her own hands. Maybe she hankered to buy a few shipping lines of her own."

Shayne said, "Turn back two or three of those clippings, Tim. During the progress of the trial. There was one story I noticed as you slid by looking for the verdict."

"Which one?" Rourke turned one clipping after another to face up to the light.

Shayne said, "There it is." It was a two-column inside-page story, headed HOUSEKEEPER TESTIFIES, and beneath it there were two pictures of a woman, side by side. The one on the left was a somewhat blurred cut of a rather pretty and slightly plump young woman standing on the front porch of a weathered frame house with a crudely painted sign over her head that said BLAIR'S BOARDING HOUSE. The caption read: *Betty Blair in front of her boarding house in Central City, Colorado.* The other picture showed the same woman some thirty years older, still smooth-faced and comely, but some twenty pounds heavier, and was captioned: *Mrs. Blair as she appeared in court today.*

Rourke nodded and said, "I was in court that day. Henrietta's attorneys called the Rogell housekeeper to testify for the plaintiff, but she was practically a hostile witness and didn't help the case much. Seems she ran a boarding house in the mining town where Rogell started his fortune, and she did testify somewhat reluctantly that people in the town still told stories about how Henrietta actually shouldered a pick in the old days right beside her brother in their first prospect tunnel. Seems they both boarded at her place in later days, and, after Mr. Blair died, John Rogell went out to Colorado and brought her back here and installed her as his housekeeper. There were a few attempts by the defense attorney to insinuate that she might have been something more than just his housekeeper, but the judge quashed those fast, ruling that he was incriminating his own witness. In the long run, the Blair testimony helped Rogell, because she was emphatic that he never denied Henrietta anything, never questioned how much money she spent or for what. There were three women on the jury," Rourke ended with a chuckle, "and you could see them drooling and wishing they were in Henrietta's shoes."

Shayne nodded and straightened up and glanced at his watch. "Tolliver has had the dog more than half an hour. Let's get back and see if there's any word."

His telephone was ringing when he unlocked the door of his apartment. He hurried to it without turning on a light, snatched it up and barked, "Hello."

Tolliver's voice answered him. "Got it, Mike."

"Got what?"

"Enough strychnine to kill a large family in that creamed chicken the Peke ate."

Shayne said exultantly, "Will Gentry will want this straight from the horse's mouth, Bud. Stay by the phone and I'll have him call you."

Timothy Rourke had switched on the light and sauntered in behind Shayne, and a wide grin came on his face when he heard Shayne's tone.

The detective gave Gentry's home telephone number to the switchboard, and told Rourke while he waited,

"You got those blisters in a good cause. Strychnine. Now we'll move."

Chief of Police Will Gentry's gruff voice came sleepily over the wire, and Shayne told him, "Bud Tolliver's got news for you, Will. About a dead dog."

"The Rogell pooch?" Gentry's voice came awake fast. "By God, Mike, I didn't think you could pull it off. What's the verdict?"

"Ask Tolliver. He's waiting for your call." Shayne gave Gentry the number. "Call me back, huh?"

"Right."

Shayne hung up and said happily, "This calls for a small libation." He poured a drink of Hennessy and waited until Rourke had put whisky in his glass. He said solemnly, "To the best grave-robber I know," and drank his off while Rourke bowed with mock humility before following suit.

His phone rang again and Will Gentry said, "Congratulations, Mike. I'm ordering an immediate P.M. on Rogell. Thank God he's slated to be cremated, so the body hasn't been embalmed."

"Can you do it without a court order or getting permission from the family?"

"With this sort of evidence, yes. In fact I discussed it with the State's Attorney after talking with you today, and got his official okay to go ahead, if things turned out this way. We'll know in the morning."

Shayne hung up and looked at his watch, his rugged face tensely alert. He muttered to Rourke, "I better call Lucy. She'll have her fingernails chewed down to the quick by this time." He lifted the phone again and gave her number.

He sat and listened to the telephone ring in her apartment, the alertness slowly fading from his face to

78

be replaced by a disbelieving frown. After the tenth ring, he broke the connection and said harshly to the hotel operator, "I'm trying to call Lucy Hamilton. Did you dial the right number?"

"I'm positive I did, Mr. Shayne. I recognized her number when you gave it. Shall I try it again?"

"Please. And make sure it's the right number."

Rourke crossed his thin legs and grinned at the worried expression on the redhead's face as the telephone again began ringing monotonously at the other end of the line.

"So maybe she's not as worried as you thought, Mike. Hell, it isn't midnight yet."

"She's at home," said Shayne fiercely. "I know how Lucy is. She knew we were making a try for the dog tonight, and she *knew* I'd phone her the first moment . . ."

He broke off as the ringing stopped and the operator asked, "Want I should keep on trying, Mr. Shayne? That's fifteen rings and she still don't answer."

Shayne said, "No," and then added quickly, "Have the operator check that number to see if anything's wrong with it."

There were deep trenches in his cheeks and his eyes were bleak as he hung up and reached for his drink.

Settled back comfortably in a deep chair, Rourke chuckled and needled him gently, "Lucy's not a teen-ager, Mike. Hell, you're acting like a heavy father. Chances are she had a date . . ."

Shayne said wrathfully, "Lucy doesn't have dates. Not when she's worried about me sticking my neck out. I'll bet my bottom dollar she's sitting beside that telephone in her apartment right now wondering why I don't call her."

Timothy Rourke shrugged his scrawny shoulders and took a long drink. "Hell, I didn't mean to imply she was stepping out on you. I just meant . . ."

The sharp ring of the telephone interrupted him. Shayne snatched it up and a cheerful voice from the hotel switchboard told him, "They checked Miss Hamilton's telephone, Mr. Shayne, and it's okay. Want me to keep on trying?"

Shayne said, "No," and slowly hung up. His hand doubled into a fist as it came away from the instrument, and the knuckles showed white. He stared down at them broodingly and Rourke didn't say anything. He lifted his head finally, and a grim smile twitched one corner of his mouth. "I guess maybe you're right, Tim. Maybe Lucy doesn't worry about me as much as I thought."

"Well, hell," said Rourke reasonably. "A gal can't be expected to sit at home alone by the telephone every night in the week just because her boss is on a case. She knows you can take care of yourself."

Shayne said, "Sure." He drained his glass and set it down slowly.

Rourke studied his friend's trenched face for a moment, cocking his head on one side and narrowing his eyes. "She didn't *say* she was going to sit at home and wait for a call, did she?"

Shayne said, "No," through clenched teeth. He got to his feet slowly and looked down at the reporter. "Don't kid me about being jealous, Tim. Lucy's a big girl like you say, and she doesn't have to get my permission to stay out until after midnight. At the same time, I'm going over to her place to see what's what. Drive me to the dock to pick up my car?"

Rourke averted his gaze from the rangy redhead's eyes, and said, "Sure." He finished his drink and unfolded himself from the deep chair.

The telephone rang again. Shayne turned back to the table and grabbed it fast. It was the clerk downstairs. "There's a Western Union messenger here, Mr. Shayne. Shall I send him up?"

Shayne said, "Yes," and exhaled a deep sigh as he dropped the receiver. He told Rourke happily, "A telegram. Lucy must have had to go out for something and knew I'd be worried. . . ." He turned and went to the door to pull it open.

Rourke chuckled aloud and said, "Why don't you two get married and have done with all this nonsense? Then you could legally chain her up every night and beat hell out of her once a week to keep her in line."

The elevator door clanged open down the hall, and jingling coins in his pocket as he waited by the open door, Shayne grinned over his shoulder and said, "Maybe I'll do that. Maybe, by God . . ."

He broke off to withdraw half a dollar from his pocket as a wizened little man appeared in the doorway wearing an oversized messenger's uniform. He intoned, "Message for Mr. Michael Shayne," and deftly exchanged a white envelope for the coin.

Shayne's expression changed as he looked down at the envelope, with his name and address penciled in crude print on the outside. He exclaimed, "Wait a minute. This isn't a telegram."

The messenger said placidly, "It sure ain't. But it's for you if you're him that's writ down there." He started to turn away, but the detective grated, "Wait a minute," as he tore the envelope open. There was a single folded sheet torn from a yellow scratchpad inside. In the same crude printing as the address, Shayne read:

You got the dog but we got your secretary. If you

81

want to see her alive again, throw the pooch in the bay and forget you ever saw her.

The message was unsigned.

Shayne grabbed the messenger's thin arm and demanded harshly, "Where did you get this?"

"Corner of Miami Avenue and Fourth. Shamrock Bar."

"Who gave it to you to bring here?"

"Bartender had it for me." The messenger twisted uneasily, dropping his rheumy gaze from Shayne's hot eyes. "Paid me two bucks and said to deliver it right away."

"How did you know to go there and pick it up?"

"Central office sent me. We get calls like that all the time. Pick up and deliver."

Shayne let go his arm and he scuttled down the hall toward the elevator.

Chapter eight

"What is it, Mike?" Rourke was beside him, his voice anxious.

Shayne extended the sheet of yellow paper wordlessly. Rourke read the brief message at a glance and swore softly. "They moved fast. Goddam it, Mike! If you hadn't been so quick on the trigger getting hold of Tolliver . . ."

"But I was quick on the trigger," said Shayne angrily. "And the autopsy's already ordered." He grabbed the sheet of yellow paper from Rourke and glared at it. "Who, in the name of God? And how did he know . . . ? Did you leave the grave open, Tim?"

"No. I filled it back in and smoothed it over the best I could in the dark. Of course, if someone went back and checked carefully . . ."

"Someone did," Shayne said. He whirled around and strode to the center table, opened the telephone book and riffled through the pages to the Rogell number. He gave it to the operator and waited for a long time with the receiver to his ear. A woman's voice finally said, "Mrs. Rogell's residence."

"This is the police," said Shayne curtly. "Sergeant Hanson speaking. I want to talk to the Rogell chauffeur. At once."

"Charles?" He was certain it was Mrs. Blair's voice.

"I'm afraid that's impossible. He's sleeping now . . . under heavy sedation."

"Wake him up then," grated Shayne. "This is the police."

"I don't care who it is," said Mrs. Blair spiritedly. "I don't believe you could wake him if you tried. Doctor gave him two pills he said would knock him out at least eight hours. He needs the rest, goodness knows. I suppose the doctor did report what happened here tonight?"

"That's why we're checking," lied Shayne. "How long ago did Charles take his pills and go to bed?"

"Right after the doctor left. I made him go out to his own apartment and tucked him in myself."

"Is Mrs. Rogell's brother still there?"

"Marvin's here, all right, but you won't get much out of him either. He didn't need any pills to pass out cold."

Shayne hung up the receiver, shaking his head at Rourke. "No help there. The housekeeper claims both Charles and the brother are dead to the world and can't be wakened."

"I been thinking, Mike. Whoever snatched Lucy and wrote this note thinks you got it before you had time to do anything with the dog. They wouldn't know about Tolliver doing a fast job for you. If you can keep them thinking that . . ."

Shayne said, "Yeh." He lifted the phone again and gave Will Gentry's home telephone number. When the chief answered, he said, "Mike Shayne again, Will. Something has come up at this end." The urgency in his voice kept Gentry from asking any questions. "Have you ordered the autopsy?"

"Sure. They should have already picked the body up from the undertaker's."

"How many people know that?"

"What do you mean?"

"Just what I asked. Can't you understand plain English?"

"Hold your water, Mike. Nobody outside the department except the undertaker, and he's sworn to secrecy. Doc Higgins promised him he'd have the corpse back in its casket tomorrow morning so no one will know."

Shayne breathed a fervent, "Thank God," and then went on strongly, "Promise me this, Will. Don't take any action tomorrow morning no matter what the P.M. says. Not till you talk to me first. Will you promise that?"

"Now, wait a minute, Mike. What gives?"

Shayne hesitated, then said flatly, "They've got Lucy. She'll stay alive as long as they think we haven't found poison inside the dog and haven't autopsied Rogell. If he can be cremated tomorrow with them still thinking that . . ."

"Lucy?" rumbled Gentry. "Who's 'they'?"

"That's what I've got to have time to find out, Will. Someone who doesn't want an autopsy on Rogell. So, for the love of God, keep it quiet, Will."

Gentry said gruffly, "I like Lucy, too. You want help?"

"That's what I don't want right now. Just complete secrecy on the autopsy . . . and a call as soon as you know."

Gentry said, "You'll have that," and Shayne hung up. He got up and said, "Drive me out to Lucy's, Tim. Maybe we can pick something up there."

The reporter hastily tossed off the last of his drink and said, "Let's go."

Downstairs, Shayne stopped at the desk to tell the clerk, "I'll be at Miss Hamilton's number in about fifteen minutes. Try her phone if anything comes up."

He got in the driver's seat of Rourke's car and headed toward Miami Avenue, explaining, "We'll stop at the Shamrock first."

"I don't get this, Mike. How could anyone get to Lucy so fast? None of the people involved know her, do they?"

"She was out there this afternoon. Charles was smart enough to figure she was my secretary, and the rest of them knew what he suspected."

"But she's not listed in the phone book. This may all be a bluff."

Shayne said, "Maybe." He was driving north on Miami Avenue, and slowed as he approached Fourth Street. A corner saloon had a sign in green neon, SHAMROCK BAR. He parked and they got out.

It was a small bar, dingy and dimly lighted. At this hour there were only three men on stools with drinks in front of them. The bartender was thin and sallow-faced, wearing a dirty white jacket. He came toward them incuriously as they ranged up against the front end of the bar, and Shayne said, "A cognac," mechanically, his gaze sliding over a row of bottles behind the bar. "Martell will be fine, with water on the side. And Grandad on the rocks."

He got out his wallet and extracted a five-dollar bill, smoothed it flat on the bar between his big hands as the bartender set their drinks in front of them. He moved the bill forward and said, "Keep the change. I want to ask you a question."

The bartender put his fingertips on the bill but did not pick it up. Pale blue eyes studied Shayne's face warily. "Sure, mister. Go ahead and ask."

"A messenger from Western Union picked up an envelope from you fifteen or twenty minutes ago. Tell me about it."

"What about it?"

"Everything."

The man shrugged, keeping the tips of his fingers on the bill, but not drawing it toward him. "There was this guy came in and busted a ten for a boiler-maker and asked could he use the phone. I said sure." The bartender jerked his head to a coin telephone on the wall behind him. "I was standing close enough to hear him ask for Western Union, and then say to send a messenger to make a pick-up from here for immediate delivery. Then he asked what the charge would be for downtown Miami, and then hung up.

"He came back to his drink, and gave me these two envelopes, see? And three ones. Said he was in a hurry and would I give the letters and the money to the messenger when he came. I said sure, and that's all there was to it."

Shayne said hoarsely, "Two envelopes?"

"Yeh. There was two. Just alike. Addressed with a pencil."

"Addressed to whom?" Shayne's voice was unnecessarily harsh, and the bartender looked at him with a touch of belligerence. "How do I know, mister? None of my business and I didn't pry. I just laid them on the cash register with the three bills, and gave 'em to the messenger when he came. Anything wrong in that?"

Shayne slowly exhaled a long-held breath. He said, "No. Nothing wrong with that. You're sure you didn't see either of the names? It would be worth twice that bill to me."

"Gee, I wisht I had." The bartender sounded truly sorry that he hadn't been more curious. "I just didn't look."

"What did the man look like?"

"Like a bum," he said promptly. "Wearing a ragged coat and needing a haircut. Thin and hungry looking.

Hell, I didn't pay no heed. Twenty-five or maybe thirty. Just a medium-looking bum."

"You never saw him in here before?"

"Sure didn't. I get a pretty good class of customers in here." The bartender glanced proudly down the bar to the trio on stools near the other end. "It's thinned out now, but half an hour ago I was pretty crowded."

"But you'd know the bum if he ever comes in again?" persisted Shayne.

The bartender screwed up his blue eyes. "I . . . reckon I might."

"If he does show his face there'll be ten bills like that in it for you if you call the police and hold him till they get here."

"Well, sure," said the man uncomfortably. "If the law wants him . . ."

Shayne said emphatically, "They do," and finished his drink.

As they got back into his car, Timothy Rourke said worriedly, "I guess that didn't help much."

"Not a damned bit. Whoever sent the note covered his tracks perfectly. Some hobo off a park bench who was delighted to earn the rest of a ten-dollar bill by having a drink in a bar and calling Western Union."

"The *notes*," Rourke reminded him emphatically as he swung around the corner and headed east on Fourth. "Who was the other one to?"

Shayne shrugged. "For you, maybe. If anyone knew you were with me tonight and it was you who did the actual grave-robbing."

"No one knew that. I swear no one saw me there."

"Lucy knew you were going with me," Shayne reminded him, and neither one of them said any more until Shayne unlocked Lucy's first-floor apartment, east of Biscayne Boulevard, with a key that Lucy had given him many years before and which he had never used until tonight.

The outer door opened directly into a long pleasant sitting room with double windows overlooking the street. There was a softly cushioned divan beneath the windows with a low coffee table in front of it. Shayne switched on an overhead light as they entered, and the two men stood close together without speaking, their eyes searching the room for any sign of disorder, any indication that Lucy had been taken away forcibly or had attempted to leave a clue as to her whereabouts behind her.

There was nothing. The room looked exactly as Shayne had seen it so many evenings in the past when he had stopped by with Lucy after a dinner together, or dropped in late to enjoy a nightcap before going on to his own bachelor quarters.

In a completely calm and exceedingly quiet voice which revealed to his old friend the intensity of the emotion he felt, Shayne said, "You stay back, Tim. I want to go through the place alone. There may be something out of place . . . something I'll recognize. . . ."

Awkwardly, Timothy Rourke said, "Sure, Mike. You go right ahead." He leaned against the door frame, digging out a cigarette and lighting it while he watched Shayne's tall frame move slowly away from him with shoulders squared and chin thrust out.

The detective noted three cigarette butts in the glass ash tray on the coffee table near the end where Lucy generally sat when they were in the apartment together. That meant a couple hours of occupancy to Shayne, indicating she had come in after a leisurely dinner and relaxed for a couple of hours before going out again. There was a single dried ring on the glass table beside the ash tray. Lucy's ingrained tidiness would never have left that ring undisturbed had she finished her drink and gone off to bed without interruption.

He moved on past the divan into the small kitchen, found everything in perfect order except for a tall glass standing on the drainboard of the sink with a small amber residue in the bottom. Again, Lucy would not have neglected to rinse out the glass and turn it upside down if she had not left hastily. He reached up a long arm and opened a cupboard across from the sink, lifted down a bottle of cognac that his secretary always kept there for him to drink from, together with a four-ounce wineglass. He emptied the warm remnants of her drink into the sink, got two ice cubes from the refrigerator and put them in the tall glass. He splashed brandy on top of them, added a modicum of tap water, and filled the wineglass nearly to the brim.

Rourke was still standing beside the door when he re-entered the sitting room. Shayne held out the tall glass and said pleasantly, "Want to gargle on this while I look at the bedroom?"

Rourke said, "Sure," and came toward him. "What do you make of it?"

"Not much this far. Lucy was here . . . alone . . . for a couple of hours after dinner. Had one drink and left in a hurry."

"Under duress?" Rourke took the drink from him, studying his face keenly.

Shayne shrugged. "I should guess not. There'd be an overturned glass . . . something to signal me. She'd know I'd be around. . . ." His voice trailed off and he took a sip of cognac, then moved to the telephone and stared down moodily at the clean white pad beside it. No telephone numbers jotted, not even a doodle. But Lucy was not the doodling kind, he reminded himself.

He went into the neat bedroom in which the only sign

of disarray or hurried departure was a pair of furry mules lying on their sides near the foot of the bed. With his intimate knowledge of Lucy's habits, Shayne knew she had changed to them immediately after coming in, had hurriedly kicked them off and put on her shoes before going out again. It was another sign of hurried departure, but not necessarily of coercion.

He went to her closet and opened it and surveyed the neat contents with bleak eyes. The array of dresses and outer wraps on hangers told him nothing, but he did note the small overnight case on the shelf above, and knew she hadn't packed for a protracted stay.

The bathroom was immaculate, as Lucy always kept it, and told him nothing more. Rourke was lounging in a deep chair when he came out, and his deep-set eyes regarded the detective with feverish brightness. "What does the master mind make of it?"

Shayne sighed and crossed to the divan where he sank down and took a long sip of cognac. "She came in alone and relaxed for an hour or so . . . then ducked out hurriedly. I don't think she had any idea what she was getting into, Tim. She'd have managed to do *something* . . . leave *some* sort of sign for me. . . ."

Lucy Hamilton's telephone rang.

Shayne's hand jerked and some of his cognac spilled on the carpet. He crossed to the instrument in two strides and said, "Hello," into the mouthpiece.

The voice that answered him was deep and strong, but undoubtedly feminine. "Is that you, Mr. Shayne?"

"Yes."

"Your hotel gave me this number. Henrietta Rogell."

Again, Shayne said, "Yes?"

"I must see you at once. At the Waldorf Towers. It's a matter I cannot discuss over the telephone."

Her voice was inflexibly determined, and Shayne

wasted no time in what he realized would be useless argument. He said, "In a few minutes, Miss Rogell," dropped the receiver and strode toward Rourke who was already on his feet draining his glass.

Without pausing on his way to the door, he said, "The Waldorf Towers, Tim. Drop me there and I'll pick up my car at the dock later."

Chapter nine

Henrietta met him at the door of her suite wearing a faded gray bathrobe cut along mannish lines and tightly belted about her lean waist, with comfortable-looking carpet slippers on her bare feet. Her grayish hair was released from its tight bun, tied behind her head with a black ribbon in a sort of pony-tail and fluffed out loosely about her face to soften the hardness of her features somewhat.

Shayne entered a pleasantly decorated and nicely furnished sitting room, and she closed the door behind him and strode past with bathrobe flapping about bare stringy ankles to a glass coffee table in front of a sofa. "I'm drinking rye," she announced, "with a smidgen of water to cut the bite. If you want some fancy mixed drink, I can call Room Service I guess."

There was a bottle of bonded rye on the coffee table beside a hotel bucket of ice cubes, a water carafe, and one highball glass. Shayne said, "Rye and water will be fine," and she went through a door at the end of the sitting room and returned with a clean glass. She handed it to him, saying, "Pour your own and I'll do the same."

The bottle was about a quarter full. Shayne poured an inch in the bottom of his glass, fished two cubes of ice out of the bucket with his fingers and dropped them in, poured water up to the halfway mark, and watched with interest while Henrietta put double that amount of whisky in her glass, added one ice cube and about a tablespoonful of water.

She then took a folded sheet of yellow paper from a pocket of her bathrobe and handed it to him. "This was delivered at the desk half an hour ago. By a Western Union messenger, they said."

Shayne read the same penciled writing as his own message:

The dog is already dead but Lucy Hamilton ain't— yet. Tell Shayne we mean business.

Henrietta sat on one end of the sofa and watched the redhead's face while he read it. "What does it mean?" she demanded. "Isn't Lucy Hamilton that nice secretary in your office?"

Shayne nodded. He got out his message and handed it to her. "Both these were given to a downtown bartender about an hour ago by a bum for delivery to us."

She read his note. "Then you did get hold of the dog?" There was a glitter of pleasure in her eyes. "As soon as you find she died from eating my poisoned creamed chicken, you can get an order delaying the funeral until they can do an autopsy on John, can't you?"

Shayne said, "If the dog *was* poisoned. If I go on and have her stomach contents analyzed."

"*If* you do," she said sharply. "Isn't that what I hired you for?"

Shayne sat down in a deep chair in front of her and crossed his long legs. He took a sip of his drink and said,

"You've read those two notes. I was in Lucy Hamilton's apartment when you phoned, and she's missing. I think I'm going to step out of this case, Miss Rogell."

"You can't. I paid you an exorbitant fee for a day's work and I have some rights in the matter. This silly note." She waved it contemptuously. "It's just a bluff to frighten you. I didn't think you were that sort."

Shayne said, "My hands are tied as long as they've got Lucy."

"Nonsense! I won't have it. I demand possession of that dog's body. I paid for it."

Shayne shook his head. "I'll return your check to-morrow."

"I'll refuse to accept it. I'll sue you. Now you listen to me, young man. . . ."

"You listen to me." He didn't raise his voice but there was a finality about his tone that checked her protest. "Your brother is dead. Lucy Hamilton is alive. I want her to stay alive. It's that simple."

"So you'll kowtow to them? Let them get away with murder just because . . ."

"Just because I may save my secretary's life by so do-ing." Shayne's voice was harsh. "Exactly. Now that you understand the situation, you can co-operate by tell-ing me anything that might help get her back. Once she's safe, I'm perfectly willing to go ahead . . . but not before."

"But the funeral is at noon. John is to be cremated and then it will be too late to do anything."

"All the more reason we should move fast to find Lucy," grated Shayne. "Who do you think wrote those notes?"

"They sound like Charles."

"That's what I thought. But I've got reason to think

95

Charles wasn't physically capable of snatching Lucy. Who else among those you suspect?"

"Any one of them. Or all of them put together. If Charles didn't write the notes, I'd guess it was someone else who tried to make them sound like Charles."

"You mean Marvin, Anita, Mrs. Blair and the doctor."

"And don't forget Harold Peabody. Cold as a fish and sharp as a hound's tooth. He's got more brains in his little finger than all the others put together. Wouldn't surprise me one little bit if he engineered the whole deal from the word go."

"What do you mean?"

"Just what I say. That he put Anita up to it from the very beginning. Fixed it for John to meet her in the first place, hoping he'd fall for her like he did. She was working in his office, you know. I don't trust that man half as far as I could throw a bull by the tail, and I've told John so hundreds of times. I think John was beginning to catch on and Peabody was scared he was going to lose John's business and that would involve a complete audit . . . and only Harold Peabody knows what an audit would show. I told John over and over that he was a fool to give Peabody a free hand with his investments and that I bet he was stealing him blind, but John trusted him. Until lately. But I think he was beginning to get suspicious and Peabody knew it. If John was pressing him for an outside audit he'd have a mighty strong motive for seeing that John died when he did."

"That motive doesn't stand up," Shayne pointed out. "With your brother's death there will be an automatic audit of his accounts and appraisal of his estate . . . for tax purposes, if nothing else. This is the one thing

Peabody would want to avoid if your suspicion is correct and there are any irregularities."

"Oh, no. Give the devil his due. The way Harold Peabody has got things fixed, he's named executor of the estate and will have his finger in whatever audit or appraisal there is. Don't think that man hasn't got every angle figured."

"What are the terms of his will?"

"Just what you might expect an old fool to do," she said acidly. "Fifty thousand to Mrs. Blair and a trust fund for me that I can only spend the interest on. The rest of it to his 'dearly beloved wife, Anita,' with no strings attached. And my trust fund also goes to her when I die."

"How much income will you have from it?"

"Oh, forty or fifty thousand a year. All right," she went on fiercely, noting the expression on his face. "Of course it's as much money as I need or can spend in a year. But that's not the point. It's the principle of it. Half that money is rightfully mine. I slaved for it back in the old days, right alongside my brother in a mine shaft. By every law in the land, I should have half of it in my own name."

"It was decided the other way when you sued for half."

"That jury," she snorted. "What could you expect? Don't tell me there's equal justice for women in this country. All they could see was that John very generously doled out whatever cash I needed."

"When you brought the suit, did you anticipate something like this?"

"John was a man . . . and I know how men are. Some little slut comes along and lifts her skirt, and he goes panting after her. That's exactly what happened when Harold Peabody fixed it for Anita to lift her skirt for my brother."

"You really think," said Shayne incredulously, "that a man with Peabody's reputation deliberately planned to introduce Anita to your brother, hoping he would marry her so that she could then murder him and gain control of his fortune?"

"I don't know anything about his reputation," she said tartly. "Do you know the man?"

"No."

"There you are. I don't say there was any definite murder plan in the beginning. I certainly do think he might have felt it would be handy to have someone like Anita married to John and exerting her influence to keep Peabody in his good graces. Then . . . if John did start getting suspicious as I think . . . well, it certainly did fix things up for Harold Peabody when John died when he did."

"And you think he's the type to pull something like this with Lucy?"

"I consider him utterly unscrupulous. If he found out you were digging the dog up to have it analyzed, I'm sure he'd stop at nothing to stop you. How *did* you find Daffy?"

Shayne said, "That's a trade secret."

"Now that you have got her body, you're not just going to sit back and do nothing because of these threats?"

"I don't intend to sacrifice Lucy's life in an effort to prove your brother was murdered." Shayne met her fiercely questioning gaze without blinking.

"Haven't you any guts at all? Or any decency. What about professional ethics? Do you have the moral right to let a murderer go free?"

Shayne sighed. "In the first place, I don't know that a murder has been committed."

"Isn't this proof enough?" She waved the yellow sheet of paper at him. "They know the dog was poisoned just

98

as I claimed all along, and they *know* that an autopsy on John will prove he was murdered. Why else would they resort to kidnaping to stop you?"

Shayne admitted, "It's pretty conclusive, but . . . so long as we don't *know* the dog was poisoned I have no moral obligation to go on and put Lucy's life in danger."

"That's quibbling," she snorted. "I thought better of you than that, Mike Shayne. How can you go on living with yourself if you weasel out this way?"

Shayne said stubbornly, "The moment Lucy is safe, I'll start moving."

"How much?" she demanded suddenly.

"How much what?"

"How much do you intend to hold me up for? I know a lot about you, Mike Shayne, and I don't believe for a minute that any woman means more to you than money. You're not *married* to the girl. She's just your secretary. Secretaries are expendable." The old spinster's face and voice were grim. "How much, Mike Shayne? I'm not a wealthy woman, but I do believe I can buy *you*. How much for immediate delivery of Daffy's body to me? Then your conscience will be clear. You can wash your hands of the whole affair and devote your entire time to getting your sniveling secretary back safe into your arms and your bed."

Shayne got up. He took a step forward and leaned down to set his half-emptied glass on the coffee table in front of Henrietta Rogell. He caught the slip of yellow paper from her fingers and carefully folded it together with the note she had given him. In a remote voice, he said, "I'll keep both of these. And I'll also keep Daffy. Good night."

He stalked out of the hotel suite and shut the door firmly behind him.

In the lobby he looked for Harold Peabody in the telephone book and found his home address in the northeast section of the city. He made a note of it and went out to a waiting cab and told the driver to take him to the fishing dock where he had left his car parked earlier that day.

Chapter ten

Peabody's address was a glittering, modern, six-story apartment building on Northeast 60th Street. Shayne parked directly in front of wide, chromium-framed glass doors flush with the sidewalk, and entered a large, softly carpeted and softly lighted lobby. He strode forward with assurance to a smartly uniformed elevator operator standing at attention outside an open cage that was also carpeted and fitted with an antique loveseat.

Shayne said, "Mr. Peabody," as he stepped inside, and the operator nodded blandly and closed the door as if it were the most natural thing in the world for Peabody to have visitors well past midnight.

They glided upward smoothly and with almost no sensation of motion, and stopped on the fourth floor. Shayne asked, "Which apartment is it?" as the door slid open, and the man nodded to a door directly across a wide hall and said, "Four A, sir."

He kept the door open and waited while Shayne stepped across to 4-A and pressed the bell. He remained waiting in the open elevator until the door opened and a plump blond girl wearing a low-cut evening gown confronted the detective. From the soundproofed apartment behind her came the sound of laughter and voices and modulated music from a hi-fi system. The girl's careful coiffure was disarranged and her lipstick was smeared. She held a champagne glass in her left hand and her blue eyes were slightly glazed as she tilted her head on one side to look up at him with approval. "Hi there, rangy, rugged and redheaded." The words were a bit slurred but had an enthusiastic lilt to them. "Where you been hiding all my life?"

Shayne said, "Just looking for you, honey," with a wide smile, and heard the elevator door close discreetly behind him.

He moved forward and she swayed against him, tilting her head farther back and closing her eyes. Shayne put his arm about her soft waist and kissed her lightly on pursed lips.

She said, "Yummy," and then giggled and linked an arm in his and led him across the small, parqueted entrance hall to an archway opening onto a large living room where a gay party was in progress.

Near a fireplace at the far side of the room, a couple were locked in a tight embrace, swaying gently to the music with their mouths glued together. Another couple were amorously entwined on a sofa at the left, and two men and a woman were seated across the room in a cluster of chairs about a table with two champagne bottles in ice buckets and trays of small sandwiches. Two of the men wore white evening jackets with cummerbunds, a third wore a conventional tuxedo, and one of the seated men was attired in white trousers and a scarlet smoking jacket. All of the girls wore evening dresses, and all of the people in the room were in varying degrees of intoxication.

The trio stopped talking and looked at them curiously as the blonde stopped Shayne in the archway and waved her champagne glass exuberantly. "See what I found, by golly. Just opened the door, believe it or not, and there he stood. Big as life and twice as ugly." She turned her head to smile at Shayne fondly. "I'm Polly, and don't you forget I saw you first."

The man in the smoking jacket got to his feet and approached them. He was in his late thirties, slender, and with a hawklike face and piercing black eyes. His expression was a curious mixture of irritation, amused affability and frank curiosity as he stopped in front of them and said to Shayne, "I don't recall . . . I don't know you, do I?"

"Who cares whether you know him or not, Harold?" said Polly gaily. "Important thing is, *I* know him. Make with the hospitality and champagne so's he can catch up a little teensy bit."

Shayne said, "You're Peabody?"

"That's right." The broker's eyes narrowed. His voice became cool and very thin. "I don't recall inviting you to this party."

Of all the people in the room, Peabody appeared to be the most sober. Indeed, Shayne's first swift impression of the man was that he was a type to carefully gauge his intake of liquor on every occasion and never allow alcohol to cloud his coldly calculating mind. It was a type Shayne disliked and distrusted, and he said in a flat voice, "I didn't know you were having a party and I'm sorry to interrupt. But there's something I'd like to discuss briefly."

"Oh, come *on*." Polly tugged at his arm. "You can't discuss anything without a drink. It isn't *decent*."

Both men disregarded her. Harold Peabody teetered forward slightly on the balls of his feet. "I can't think of anything that needs discussion at this hour. I think you'd better go."

The detective said, "My name is Shayne, Mr. Peabody. Michael Shayne."

There was not a flicker of expression on the thinly

arrogant features in front of him to indicate that the name meant anything to Peabody. But he said decisively, "I can think of nothing I wish to discuss with a private detective. Certainly not here and at this hour. If you wish to call my secretary in the morning for an appointment . . ."

Shayne shook his red head slowly. "I want some answers now. If we could step into another room . . . ?"

"Gee, golly, gosh!" exclaimed Polly loudly, so everyone in the room turned to listen. "A real live private eye. Mike Shayne, no less. Anybody know where the body's hid?"

Peabody lifted one slender, well-manicured hand in a gesture of annoyance. He said stiffly, "Control yourself, Polly. If you insist, Mr. Shayne . . ." He turned to a hallway leading to the left, and Shayne smiled down at Polly and disengaged her hand from his arm. "Sorry, darling, but duty calls. *You* have that drink. Have two of them," he added generously as he followed his reluctant host down the hall and into a small study.

"Now then," said Peabody, closing the door firmly, "please explain this unwarranted intrusion."

Shayne said roughly, "Come off your high horse, Peabody. You know why I'm here as well as I do."

The broker did not reply. He stood very stiff and still, waiting for the detective to go on.

"Are you going to deny," demanded Shayne hotly, "that you know Miss Rogell retained me today to investigate her brother's death?"

A faintly contemptuous smile twitched Peabody's tight lips. "I don't feel myself under any obligation to either deny or confirm anything, Mr. Shayne."

"The hell you say. This is a murder investigation, Peabody."

"Murder? May I ask who the victim is?"

"Miss Rogell is certain her brother was murdered."

"I was present at the time of his death," Peabody pointed out coldly. "I was there when his own doctor signed a death certificate stating his demise was due to natural causes. I am also fully aware that our excellent police department made careful investigation into the circumstances of John Rogell's death and are completely satisfied with their results. This hardly adds up to murder in my lexicon."

"What about the bereaved widow's pet bitch?" demanded Shayne.

"Ah, yes. Daffy. A most unpleasant little creature. What about her?"

"I don't believe anyone signed a death certificate for her."

"But there was another thorough police investigation," Peabody reminded him acidly. "With the same negative results. See here," he went on impatiently. "I have guests in the other room. I suggest you investigate and be damned, but I fail to see that it is any concern of mine."

"You know I've got Daffy's body," Shayne challenged. "And if it is proved that the dog died from a dose of poison intended for Miss Rogell, it will be accepted as prima-facie evidence that the attempt was made on her life because she refused to accept the findings on her brother. An autopsy on John Rogell will then be a foregone conclusion."

"I know nothing of the sort," said Peabody indifferently. "I understood that Daffy had been interred and that Mrs. Rogell . . . quite properly in my opinion . . . refused to have the body of her pet desecrated to satisfy an old woman's obviously absurd suspicions."

Shayne said harshly, "I think you're lying, Peabody. Don't tell me Anita didn't get on the phone to you the moment she discovered Daffy had been dug up."

"I don't intend to stand here and be insulted in my own home," said Peabody. "Leave immediately or I'll call the police and ledge a formal complaint."

Shayne slapped him. The force of his openhanded blow rocked the broker sideways and he staggered to keep his footing. Shayne's eyes were blazing as his right hand shot out and grabbed the scarlet lapels of the smoking jacket tightly at Peabody's throat and jerked him upright.

"Lodge all the goddam complaints you want," he grated. "But listen to one thing, Peabody, and pass the word along to anybody else who may be interested." He lifted the broker off the floor and shook him viciously and Peabody's face went ashen and he made gurgling noises in his throat.

"If anything happens to Lucy Hamilton, I'll kill the man who's responsible. Personally, and with distinct pleasure. I don't know whether it was your idea or not, but if it was, it was the worst goddam mistake you ever made. Tell Anita and Charles and all the rest of them that." He flung Peabody back angrily and the broker crashed into a desk behind him.

Shayne turned and jerked the door open and stalked out of the study. He looked neither to right nor left as he strode through the end of the living room and out the entryway. He slammed the outer door behind him and stabbed viciously at the elevator button, frustrated rage mingling with the realization that he had been utterly childish in his handling of the situation.

The black mood stayed with him while he drove to his hotel and went up to his corner suite. There was nothing he could do now except wait for a report from

Will Gentry. He was morally certain what the report would be, and he shrank from the decision he would have to make if it was determined that Rogell had been murdered.

The glasses and bottles were on the center table where he and Rourke had left them, and Shayne put the whisky bottle back on the shelf, went into the kitchen and rinsed out the tall glass Rourke had drunk from, put ice cubes in it and filled it with water.

Back in the living room he filled his smaller glass with cognac and settled back with a cigarette, taking alternate sips of liquor and ice water while his brooding gaze moved restlessly about the familiar room and his thoughts went over and over the personalities involved in the Rogell case, seeking some clue to a course of action that would insure Lucy's safety.

The telephone rang beside him before he had half finished his drink. He lifted it on the first ring and said, "Hello."

Lucy Hamilton's voice came over the wire, without the familiar lilt in it, but calm and steady and purposeful:

"Michael. Just listen to me and don't ask questions. I'm *all right*. I'll be all right if you drop the Rogell case . . . don't have the dog's stomach analyzed. I will be released tomorrow afternoon if the funeral goes off on schedule." Her calm rendition of prepared lines changed to staccato intensity. "Don't pay any attention . . ."

There was a click and then silence. Shayne's hand was unsteady as he replaced the receiver. Subconsciously, he had expected her call. Whoever was holding Lucy would be smart enough to know the only pressure that could be exerted on the detective would be his belief that she was safe and would be released safely if he followed orders. On the other hand, how many kidnap victims *were* returned safe after the ransom was paid?

Shayne's big hand gripped the wineglass with white-knuckled force as he slowly drained it without taking it from his lips. He sat looking at the empty glass for a long moment and his other hand stretched out mechanically toward the bottle. He arrested the motion in mid-air, shook his head from side to side and deliberately drew back his arm and threw the glass across the room where it shattered against the wall.

He knew there would be no sleep for him that night. And he didn't want any more liquor just then. There was nothing in the world he could do about Lucy, yet he had to do something. He couldn't sit there comfortably for hours with only the company of his own thoughts. If he did, he'd go on drinking. And he didn't want that.

He got up and paced restlessly up and down the room. He should, of course, take the kidnap notes to Will Gentry at once—throw the entire resources of the police department into the search for her and her abductor.

But he knew he wasn't going to do that. Once the alarm was out, Lucy's life wouldn't be worth a plugged nickel. Alone, he could accomplish exactly as much as the police department. Which was exactly nothing.

Yet he knew he had to try. He couldn't just sit and wait for the autopsy report. He was already positive in his own mind that the finding would be murder. There was no other possible reason for Lucy being snatched.

If there were only some point of departure. Some end that he could pick up with a faint hope of unraveling the knot.

He stopped his restless pacing, got the two notes out of his pocket and read them both again. The one point of contact was the bum who had delivered the notes to the Shamrock bartender. Let's see, now. He came in with a ten-dollar bill that he broke by buying a boiler-maker. That would be about eighty cents in a place like the Shamrock. Another dime for the phone call to Western Union. And three dollars left behind to pay the messenger. That left the guy six dollars profit from the transaction.

Wait a minute, though! Where was the man who had given him the notes and the ten-dollar bill while he was in the barroom? It stood to reason they must be complete strangers. The only safe way to handle a thing like that was to cruise around and pick up a man off the street who had never seen you before and couldn't possibly put the finger on you if he was apprehended. So, how would you know you could trust such a bum to carry out his part of the bargain and spend three of the precious ten dollars to get the notes delivered?

The obvious answer was that you wouldn't trust him. Not completely. You'd take him to a joint like the Shamrock and send him inside with explicit instructions, and you'd go in behind him and unobtrusively have a drink at the bar while you watched him call Western Union and made sure he left the money and the notes behind. Or, at the very least, you'd hang around outside to be sure he carried out your orders.

Shayne had his coat on and was headed toward the door by the time he got that far in his theorizing.

The Shamrock was still open when he got there the second time. The same bartender was still listlessly on duty, and now there were five bar-stools occupied, two of them by women who were giggling with three men eager to buy them drinks.

The bartender recognized the redhead, and glanced inquiringly toward the bottle of cognac behind him. Shayne nodded and the man poured out a drink and remembered to put a glass of water beside it. He leaned his forearms on the bar and asked, "You get a line on that fellow you was asking about?"

Shayne shook his head. "That's why I'm back. To see if you can remember another damned thing about him that might help."

"Sorry, mister. I told you all I could the first time."

"Something else has occurred to me. How busy were you at the time he was in here? Take your time and think back carefully," urged Shayne. "Was business light or heavy?"

"Medium, sorta, I guess." The bartender wrinkled his forehead. "About that time of night we get a pretty good crowd. Regulars, mostly."

"I remember you said that," Shayne encouraged him. "So, maybe you might have noticed a stranger that came in about the same time the bum did. Stayed for a drink or two while he was here, and then went out after he left."

"See what you mean," mumbled the bartender, wrinkling his forehead deeper and half closing his eyes in deep concentration. "Another guy keeping an eye on him, sorta, to make sure he called Western Union and the notes got left with me?"

"That's it exactly. Keep this up and I'll get you a detective rating on the police force."

Obviously pleased, the man continued his effort to concentrate while Shayne sipped at his drink and waited hopefully. Finally, he shook his head. "It just don't come. I been thinking back hard, but it just don't come, mister. There was a pretty good crowd in here. Some that I never saw before. But I don't recollect any one of 'em paying any particular heed to this bum."

"Keep on thinking," Shayne urged him. "Here's a couple of descriptions." He described Charles first, ending, "You'd have noticed him for sure. Two front

110

teeth freshly knocked out and the side of his face split, with probably a bandage on it."

The man shook his head decisively. "I'd remember him for sure. Nobody like that."

Shayne said without much hope, "Try these two on for size." He described Harold Peabody and Marvin Dale as best he could, realizing as he did so how commonplace both were, and how unlikely to arouse any particular notice from a busy bartender.

When the man again shook his head regretfully, Shayne finished his drink briskly and shoved a five across the counter. "Thanks for trying. Let's take one more crack at it from another direction. You said the fellow was maybe twenty-five or thirty and needed a haircut. Wearing a ragged coat and hungry-looking. *How* hungry-looking?"

"Jeez, I dunno." The bartender waved his hands vaguely. "You know how it is. Just in a manner of speaking, I guess."

"What I mean," said Shayne carefully, "is whether he looked like a man that needed a square meal more than a flop for the night. We know he walked out of here with about six bucks," he explained. "I'm trying to put myself in his position and guess what direction he'd head in. With six bucks to spend. More liquor?" Shayne shook his head slowly. "He could have got that right here as well as some place else. Food . . . or a flop?"

"With six dollars, he could buy both right here on Miami Avenue," the bartender told him. "Plenty places up the street he could fill his belly for a buck or two. Beds for a dollar up."

Shayne nodded grimly. He knew it was hopeless. From the beginning he had realized it was useless to hope he could trace the man after he walked away from the Shamrock with a boiler-maker under his belt and six dollars in hand. But he still had to try. There were empty hours of the night still stretching out in front of him, and he'd be happier doing something instead of sitting at home waiting for another day.

So he tried.

He left his car parked in front of the Shamrock and took the east side of Miami Avenue first, working his way northward for six blocks, stopping at every hole-in-the-wall eating or drinking joint, stubbornly climbing up one or two flights of stairs at every cheap hotel, repeating his queries over and over again and getting the same negative replies.

Six blocks north, he crossed to the west side and worked his way back, passing the Shamrock on the opposite side of the Avenue and continuing south to Flagler. There, he went to the east side again, and back to the Shamrock. It was full daylight by the time he completed the full circuit, and all the bars and eateries were closed.

It was still much too early to do anything else, so he turned to the right on Fourth Street and continued his canvass of the rooming houses on the south side of the street for three blocks, and then back on the north side across the Avenue for three blocks and then back on the other side to his parked car.

It was after seven o'clock when he got behind the steering wheel again and drove back to his hotel. His face was gaunt with exhaustion and his eyes red-rimmed with lack of sleep, and he had accomplished exactly nothing.

But he had tried.

Back in his own room, he walked past the cognac bottle on the center table into the small kitchen and put a teakettle of water to heat. He measured six heaping tablespoons of finely ground coffee into the top of a

112

dripolator, waited beside the stove until the water boiled, and poured the top of the drip-pot full. Then he went into the bathroom, shedding clothes as he went, shaved carefully and took a stinging hot shower, following it with the coldest water that Miami offered.

Then he sat down in the living room with a mug of strong black coffee and waited for his telephone to ring.

Chapter eleven

He dressed in fresh clothes while he waited, and when the telephone finally did ring it was Will Gentry as he anticipated.

"I just got the autopsy report, Mike."

"And?"

"John Rogell died of heart failure."

The tenseness went out of Shayne and he clawed at his red hair unhappily.

"No question about it?"

"None whatever. Doc Higgins did a complete and careful job. Rogell's heart just stopped beating . . . as Doctor Jenson had warned him it might do if he married a young woman at his age and with his heart condition."

Shayne said, "Then why in hell did someone try to feed Henrietta strychnine . . . and kidnap Lucy to try and prevent the autopsy?"

Gentry said soberly, "Forgive me for kidding about it, Mike. He did die because his heart stopped beating . . . on account of he ingested at least a teaspoonful of tincture of digitalis within half an hour before he died."

Shayne said, "Goddam it, Will . . ."

"All right. I apologize. I know how worried you are about Lucy. Still nothing on her?"

"I had a telephone call from her last night . . . to say she was okay and would be okay if the autopsy weren't done and the funeral went off without any hitch."

"Do you believe it, Mike?"

"As much as I believe any goddam kidnaper." Shayne's voice was harsh with strain. "Who knows about the autopsy?"

"Doc Higgins and I . . . and the undertaker."

"You know the undertaker personally?"

"Not personally, but it was put to him in no uncertain terms last night that *no* one was to suspect the body had left his place. He'll be in court charged with hampering a homicide investigation if it leaks out . . . and he knows it. I think we're safe on that score, Mike. Rogell is back in his coffin and there's no reason on God's earth why he shouldn't be cremated at noon with no one being the wiser."

Shayne said, "Thanks, Will."

"Hell, I'm as worried about Lucy as you are. On the other hand, Mike . . . now we've got definite proof Rogell was murdered by someone in the house that evening. We'll work as quickly as possible, but . . ."

"Tell me about the digitalis," Shayne interrupted. "Isn't that a regular medicine for the heart?"

"Sure. Rogell had been on the stuff for years. A daily dose of twelve drops had been keeping him alive. Doctor Jenson prescribed it first, and the new fellow . . . Evans . . . kept the dosage the same. Everyone knew he had to have his twelve drops daily, and that's probably why they used the stuff to kill him . . . hoping the extra amount wouldn't be noticed if there was an autopsy."

"How many people would have known a teaspoonful would be deadly?"

"Probably everyone who had anything to do with his care. Higgins says they would have been warned the dose had to be measured very accurately . . . that an excess amount would be dangerous to a man in his condition."

"And the manner of death?" queried Shayne sharply. "Would that match Evans's diagnosis and his death certificate?"

"Exactly. Higgins admits he would have signed the death certificate himself under those same circumstances. He attaches no blame to Evans."

"How could they get the old man to take so large a dose?"

"That was the easiest part of it, Mike. Here's the complete picture as we have it now. His wife always administered the twelve drops personally about midnight before he went to sleep. She gave it to him in a cup of hot chocolate milk which the housekeeper prepared in the kitchen each evening and put in a thermos jug downstairs before she retired. This would have been common household knowledge, of course. The medicine bottle was kept in the bathroom shared by Rogell and his wife. Anita could have poured an extra teaspoonful in his milk on that particular night . . . or just about anyone else in the house could have got hold of the bottle and slipped it into the thermos jug downstairs."

"That leaves it nice and wide open," said Shayne bitterly.

"Right. Now I want to know what in hell you're doing about Lucy."

Shayne said, "I've got to talk to you, Will. Don't make a move until I see you. And can you have the detectives on tap who went out to Rogell's that night?"

"I will. But, Mike! Don't expect me to sit on this.

We've got a poisoner who has killed once, and made a second attempt."

"And he or she has got Lucy," Shayne reminded him grimly.

Gentry said with heavy finality, "I'll be waiting for you in my office," and hung up.

As the result of a telephone call, Timothy Rourke met the detective at a side entrance to police headquarters. They paused outside while Shayne briefly explained the latest developments to Rourke, and then they went in to Gentry's private office together.

The Miami Chief of Police was a solid man, with square, rugged features that were the color of raw beef. He had a thick black cigar in his mouth, and he bit down on it hard when he saw the redhead's companion. "What the hell, Mike? I thought you were anxious to keep this thing quiet."

Shayne said, "Tim's got to be in on it. He already is. He dug up Daffy last night and was with me when I got Bud Tolliver's report. And he knows about Lucy, too. He won't print anything."

"It's up to you," Gentry conceded. "Now, what is this about Lucy? Give it to me straight."

Shayne got out the two sheets of yellow paper and laid them in front of Gentry. "These were delivered to me and Miss Henrietta about midnight last night. By a messenger who'd picked them up at a Miami Avenue bar." He went on to describe their visit to the Shamrock Bar while Will Gentry read the two notes.

"I went straight to Lucy's place, Will, and found she'd been there a couple of hours during the evening . . . probably after dinner . . . and had left hurriedly. I'm sure she didn't know *why* she was leaving because there was nothing left for me. Then there was the phone call from her later that I told you about."

Chief Gentry had curiously rumpled eyelids which he habitually raised and lowered much in the manner of venetian blinds. He leaned back in his chair and folded them up as he demanded, "Who out at the Rogell place knew you had dug up the dog's body. How did they know *you* did it . . . and how to get at Lucy?"

Shayne lit a cigarette and briefly recounted the ruse he had employed to discover where Daffy was buried, and how he and Tim had gotten possession of the body.

"They guessed why I was there at night, of course," he concluded, "and after I left with Dr. Evans somebody must have checked Daffy's grave. How they knew how to get to Lucy, I don't know. But someone was desperate enough to kidnap her to try and stop me from having the dog's stomach contents analyzed."

"The chauffeur sounds most likely," rumbled Gentry.

"I know. The two notes sound like him. But I knocked hell out of him, Will, and Mrs. Blair swears he went to bed at once in his own room over the garage with a sedative strong enough to put him out for eight hours."

"The widow and her brother?" demanded Gentry.

"I swear I don't know. The brother appears weak, and was pretty drunk. Anita is . . . capable of anything. On the other hand, Henrietta plugs for Harold Peabody as the master mind. And I wouldn't put anything past the cold-blooded bastard," Shayne went on angrily. He described his brief visit to the broker's apartment. "I suppose the party gives him a sort of alibi, although I wouldn't suspect him of personally pulling a snatch anyhow. I think he's perfectly capable of arranging such a job though. But guessing is no good," he went on somberly. "Someone has Lucy put away on ice, and all we can hope right now is that they think I'm sufficiently scared to not have the dog analyzed."

Gentry leaned back with a sigh and rolled his sodden cigar from one corner of his mouth to the other. "You think she'll be safe as long as they think that?"

"Until after the funeral anyhow." Shayne met his gaze squarely. "If you don't upset the applecart by doing anything to indicate the Rogell case is being reopened."

"And after the funeral?"

Shayne shook his red head and said doggedly, "If it goes off all right and the killer thinks Rogell is safely cremated and all proof of murder has gone up in smoke, I think there's a chance Lucy will be released."

"Or?" asked Gentry significantly.

"Or killed," Shayne said bluntly, the trenches deep in his cheeks. "But they'll keep her safe until after the funeral, Will, and I want that much time with no official interference."

"You're asking me to sit on a murder."

"A murder you wouldn't know a damned thing about if I hadn't handed it to you on a silver platter," flared Shayne.

Gentry said soothingly, "Sure, Mike. I grant you that. Sure, I'll give you all the time you want," he added generously. "Up until . . . say . . . three o'clock this afternoon."

"That ought to be plenty," said Shayne bitterly, "for me to solve a murder that the whole goddam police force of Miami has had in their lap for several days." He got up and demanded abruptly, "Where'll I find Petrie and Donovan?"

"They're waiting for you right inside." Will Gentry gestured toward a closed door. "I've told them to give you everything, Mike, and in addition to that, they're under your orders if you want to make use of them."

"Until three o'clock?"

Gentry said, "Until three o'clock," and Shayne jerked his head at Rourke and went to the side door to interview the two detectives who had handled the Rogell investigation.

Chapter twelve

Shayne and Rourke both knew the two city detectives casually, and the men greeted them without particular enthusiasm as they entered. Petrie was thin and sour-faced, and he said sneeringly, "Gentry tells us you're going to turn the Rogell thing into murder . . . and then solve it for us."

Donovan was flabby-fat and easy-going. He grinned amiably and told them, "Don't pay no heed to Jim. He's sore because the chief wouldn't let him haul in that hot little dish of a widow and give her a going-over. Not that I wouldn't like to work over her myself, if you get what I mean." He rolled his eyes and smacked his lips suggestively. "Like the guy comes home from the office and when the wife complains about all the work she's did that day, he says, 'What about me, doggone it? Slaving in the office over a hot secretary all day.' "

Shayne said, "Ha-ha. Why don't you two start by telling us exactly what happened the night Rogell died."

With Petrie doing most of the talking and Donovan filling in some details, they related how they had been called to the Rogell house by an insistent telephone call received from his sister at twelve-forty, which was exactly eleven minutes after her millionaire brother had died quietly in his bed.

On arrival, they had been met at the door by Henrietta, fully clothed and tearless, loudly insisting that she was convinced John Rogell had been poisoned by his wife. In the small library off the right of the hall, they had found Marvin Dale, soddenly drunk and obviously quite pleased that his brother-in-law had passed on. With Marvin had been Harold Peabody, sober and shaken, who told them he had spent the latter part of the evening alone with the millionaire in his second-floor sitting room, going over business affairs with him until Anita had interrupted them precisely at midnight with a hot drink for her husband which she invariably brought to him each night at that hour.

It had been a normal evening, Peabody insisted, with Rogell in the best of spirits and apparently in perfect physical condition, and he had left husband and wife together at twelve with no premonition of what was to come, had paused in the library for a nightcap with Marvin, and they were together when Anita called down frantically that John had had a stroke and to call Dr. Evans immediately.

The doctor had arrived within ten minutes and found his patient already dead. He was upstairs with the body when the detectives went up, and had not the slightest hesitancy in positively declaring that death was the normal result of Rogell's heart condition, and had signed the death certificate to that effect.

Mrs. Blair, the housekeeper, had been in Anita's boudoir consoling the grief-stricken widow whom they found fetchingly attired in a lacy nightgown and filmy black negligee. Mrs. Blair was also wearing slippers and robe, and told the officers she had retired to her third-floor quarters about eleven as was her custom, after preparing a silver thermos pitcher of hot chocolate milk

122

for Mr. Rogell and leaving it downstairs on a tray on the dining table for Anita to take up to him at midnight, a nightly service which she insisted on performing for him herself every night.

In a highly emotional state and with much sobbing, Anita had related how John had appeared in good spirits when she entered the room with his tray and shooed Peabody out. Her husband was already in pajamas and robe, she told them, and she poured out his hot drink herself and sat with him while he drank it. Then she had gone into his separate bedroom with him (they occupied adjoining suites with a large connecting bath) and there was some indication, in halting testimony, that they might have been preparing to have intercourse when he suddenly groaned and stiffened in his bed, and a moment later his body became rigid and his breathing shallow and fast. It was then she had run to the head of the stairs to shout for the doctor, and when she returned to the bedroom a moment later, she could no longer detect his breathing. Henrietta had then come in from her own suite at the end of the hallway, and angrily berated her for being an unfaithful wife, then gone on to an open accusation of murder.

The officers had also interviewed Charles, who told them he had been in his quarters above the garage reading a magazine until about ten when he had come to the kitchen for a snack and had chatted with Mrs. Blair for a time while she was preparing Mr. Rogell's hot chocolate milk. He had returned to his apartment and was in bed when he heard the excitement in the big house and realized that something was wrong.

That, in essence, was the contents of the report Petrie and Donovan had made of their investigation. Discounting Henrietta's almost hysterical accusations, there was nothing whatsoever to indicate that John Rogell had not died a perfectly natural death. But as he discussed the case with the two detectives, after reading their report, Shayne discovered they had not been altogether as wholly satisfied as the report indicated. There was definite agreement between them that it was quite possible Anita's grief was not as genuine as she tried to make it appear. Little things they had noticed, including a certain change in her manner when she looked at Charles and spoke to him for the first time since she had become a widow. Nothing you could put your finger on, they explained, but you got a feeling of, at least, a sort of relief between the two of them that it was all over.

They pointed out, however, that this did not necessarily mean they were guilty of anything more than possibly having had some sort of affair under the old man's nose. Certainly it was nothing on which to base a suspicion of murder.

Also, while trying to interview Marvin Dale in his drunken condition, he had openly admitted his pleasure in Rogell's death, muttering that things would be different around the house now, and strongly intimating that his sister's millionaire husband had disapproved of his sponging on her and had practically ordered her to cease providing him with funds.

And, of course, there was Henrietta. But you could see that her nose was completely out of joint and that she deeply resented Anita and would stop at nothing to harm her.

So there you were, the detectives said, and how in hell can you make murder out of any of that?

They had turned in a shorter report on the death of Daffy. Again they had been sent to the Rogell house after an almost hysterical call from Henrietta insisting that this time someone had tried to murder her. Again they had found exactly the same group of people present, with Marvin a little more sober and slightly more coherent this time, and all of them somewhat drawn together and somewhat on the defensive, as they related Henrietta's impassioned harangue shortly before dinner, during which she had accused them all, singly or in unholy conspiracy, of having poisoned her brother. She had warned them flatly that she was going to demand an autopsy on John's body, and was prepared to take whatever legal measures were necessary to force such action.

Then they had sat down at the dining table for dinner together and Henrietta had been served her special plate of creamed chicken from a chafing dish that had stood on the sideboard for half an hour, the others all sharing a dish of curried shrimp because Henrietta's allergy to seafood was well known to all.

None of them at the table, it appeared, had noticed Henrietta when she surreptitiously removed some of her chicken to a saucer and put it down on the floor beside her for Daffy. Indeed, Anita had insisted that she had done no such thing, and Peabody was quietly dubious as to whether she could have done so without being noticed . . . but anyhow the little dog had had convulsions and died almost at once . . . and Henrietta insisted she *hadn't* eaten any of her chicken.

But the last scrap of it had vanished by the time the officers arrived, and even the chafing dish and Henrietta's plate and the dog's saucer had been washed clean.

Sure, that looked suspicious, they both agreed, but you had to blame Mrs. Blair for it because it appeared no one had ordered her to do so, and it was pretty hard to suspect the plump and pleasant housekeeper of murder and attempted murder.

But the swift burial of Daffy was a somewhat different matter. All of the witnesses agreed that Anita had become hysterical after her pet's death, and called Charles in and ordered him to take Daffy's dead body away from her sight and bury the bitch at once. Her explanation of this somewhat suspicious action was that she had a deep-rooted phobia about death and corpses and could not stand the sight or thought of them.

But when the detectives pointed out that it would clarify matters and either prove or disprove Henrietta's contention that her chicken had been poisoned if they could take the dog's body for analysis, Anita had arrogantly denied the need to disprove Henrietta's absurd charge, and had flatly ordered Charles not to show the detectives where Daffy was buried.

"So, there you have it," Petrie summed up the situation with a shrug. "Sure, it looked suspicious but we couldn't force them to show us the dog's grave. Maybe we could have taken it into court and got a search warrant, but Will Gentry didn't think so."

Shayne nodded thoughtfully and said, "Let's go back to Rogell's death. Check your report and read me exactly what Peabody said about his leaving the couple together upstairs."

Petrie shuffled some typewritten pages clipped together and said, "Let's see. Here it is." He cleared his throat and began reading:

"Mr. Rogell and I concluded our business shortly before midnight and were smoking a final cigar when Mrs. Rogell came in from the bathroom, carrying a thermos jug and a cup, and a bottle containing her husband's heart medicine which I knew he took every night. She

126

was dressed in a negligée, and was very sweet, but wifely and firm, when she insisted it was time for John's medicine and I would have to go. She put the cup and jug on a bedside table, and measured out his medicine with an eye-dropper into the cup. I said good night to them both and went out while she was pouring hot chocolate into the cup."

Petrie stopped and looked up. "Want me to go on?"

Shayne said, "No. But I do want to get it straight in my mind about that thermos jug. The way I understand it, Mrs. Blair fixed the chocolate drink in the kitchen as was her custom, and left it on the dining table about eleven o'clock before she retired."

"That's the way she told it," Donovan said. "They all said she did it that way every night, and that it was understood Anita would take it up at midnight and give the old man his daily dose of medicine . . . and from some other things that was said we got the idea she was maybe gonna give him his daily dose of something else along with it." He snickered. "Isn't that right, Jim?"

"Yeh. She'd be the one to do that little thing . . . just in case the chauffeur didn't give her all she wanted." Petrie looked at Shayne. "You're thinking there might have been something else in his cup of hot milk besides medicine?"

Shayne said, "He died half an hour after drinking it. It would have been smart to grab the jug and the cup he drank from and have them analyzed."

"But that doctor swore there was nothing to indicate poisoning. Said it was exactly the way he had expected the old boy to kick off."

"But you did have Henrietta screaming murder," Shayne reminded him mildly.

"That old biddy," snorted Donovan. "You could see

127

she plumb hated Anita's guts, and you don't pay much heed to that kind of raving."

Shayne said, "I'm not blaming you boys. But it's different with me. I've got a big fat fee riding on the offchance I can prove it was murder. And the way it stacks up . . . anybody in the house that evening had the opportunity to put something in the thermos jug while it was sitting on the dining table downstairs."

"Except maybe Henrietta, the way I remember it," said Petrie doubtfully. "And Peabody, too. I don't remember whether he mentioned leaving the old man's room during that hour or not. Do you, Terance?"

"I don't think he mentioned it one way or the other. But he wouldn't of, of course, if he had slipped out of Rogell's room and downstairs to poison his milk."

Petrie was flipping through the pages of the typewritten report again, pausing to glance at a paragraph, and then turning on.

"Right here, Peabody says, 'I was with Mr. Rogell in his upstairs sitting room from ten o'clock until midnight when Mrs. Rogell came in, and we were undisturbed during that period.'"

"So that don't prove nothing," Donovan pointed out again. "Rogell ain't alive to say it ain't so."

"Here's Henrietta," said Petrie, reading, "'I retired to my own suite about ten-thirty. Mrs. Blair and Charles were in the kitchen where she was warming John's midnight milk. I heard Mrs. Blair come up about half an hour later, and I stepped out in the hallway to intercept her and ask if I might accompany her up to the third floor to get a book which she had promised to lend me. We went up together, and I remained with her, talking, until we heard Anita screeching that

128

John was dying. We hurried down together and found John . . .' "

Petrie broke off. "That takes care of her during the hour the jug sat on the dining table. And the housekeeper, too, because Mrs. Blair corroborated Henrietta's story exactly."

"But she could have put something in the milk when she fixed it. Before she went up at eleven," Timothy Rourke pointed out.

Shayne said, "Right. And so could Charles have slipped something in the jug while he was in the kitchen and Mrs. Blair was busy. And Anita and Marvin were downstairs together during the hour before midnight. Counting Peabody, who could have left Rogell for a time, we have five people who had access to the jug of hot milk before Rogell drank it."

"What's the use kicking it around now?" demanded Petrie. "The old boy is going to be burned to a crisp at noon, and if there ever was any evidence of murder inside him, it'll be destroyed."

"That's why we've got to move fast," said Shayne with a driving intensity behind his words. He glanced at his watch and calculated swiftly that it was just a few minutes before eight o'clock in Denver, Colorado. He dragged a worn address book from his pocket and checked an old entry, then told the others, "Sit tight right here. I'm going to make a fast phone call from Gentry's office, and then we'll all get on our horses."

He strode through the connecting door and found Gentry talking to a young patrolman who stood stiffly at attention beside the chief's desk. Shayne said, "I've got to make a call, Will," picked up a telephone from his desk and got the police operator. He said crisply, "Person-to-person in Denver, Colorado. Felix Ritter.

129

Here's an old telephone number I have for him." He read the number from his book and lowered one hip to the corner of Gentry's desk while he waited. Impersonally, and with only a tiny part of his mind, he listened to Chief Gentry chewing out the patrolman for some minor infraction of regulations while the long-distance connection was being made, and when he heard Ritter's voice on the other end, he said incisively, "Mike Shayne in Miami, Felix. Can you get out to Central City fast?"

"Mike? Sure I can. There's a new road since you were here, and . . ."

"Fast as you can make it," interrupted Shayne. "Write this down. I want any gossip or scandal from the natives about a Mrs. Betty Blair who used to run a rooming house there where the millionaire miner, John Rogell, hung out while he was making his fortune. Find out how friendly they were in the old days . . . and what people thought when Mr. Blair died and the widow came to Miami to work as John Rogell's housekeeper. Got it? Here's an angle. He left her fifty thousand bucks in his will."

"Sure, Mike. Rogell just died, huh? In Miami? Remember reading how he got his start in Central City."

"Fast as you can make it, Felix. I need any damned thing you can pick up and relay to me by twelve o'clock. Make a collect call to the Chief of Police here. Will Gentry. Before noon."

Felix Ritter in Denver said, "Will do," and Shayne hung up. The patrolman was on his way out, and Shayne told Gentry, "You'll be getting a call about Mrs. Blair from Central City before noon. I'll be checking with you . . ."

Another telephone on Gentry's desk interrupted him.

The chief scooped it up and said, "Yes?" He listened a moment, lifting a beefy hand at Shayne, his rumpled eyelids moving up and down slowly. He hung up and told Shayne, "Let's get out to the Rogell place with Petrie and Donovan. Marvin Dale committed suicide out there last night. And left a suicide note addressed to you."

Chapter thirteen

In Shayne's car, he and Rourke followed the screaming siren of Chief Gentry's limousine through downtown
traffic and out Brickell Boulevard to the Rogell estate.
There were no other cars parked in front of the house,
and the two men trotted up the stairs and across the
porch behind the chief and his two detectives.

A white-faced maid opened the door for them immediately, and Mrs. Blair hovered in the wide hallway
behind her, wringing her hands and with tear streaks on
her broad face.

"This way," she directed them. "Up the stairs here. I
just can't believe it. Poor Mr. Dale. Who'd ever have
thought he'd do a terrible thing like this?"

The five men trooped beside her silently up the curving stairway where she turned to the right to an open
doorway with Charles standing in front of it. He was in
his shirtsleeves and without a tie, his hair uncombed and
a heavy growth of dark stubble on his square face. There
was a bluish bruise on his cheekbone and a pad of
gauze on the side of his mouth under a piece of surgical
tape. He kept his lips pressed tightly together and his

eyes had a sullen glare when he saw Shayne with the others. He stepped aside from the doorway without speaking, and they entered a medium-sized bedroom with the body of Marvin Dale sprawled on the floor in front of a drop-leaf table with an overturned straight chair beside him.

The young man's face was twisted and ghastly in death, his body stiffly contorted, indicating that he had writhed agonizingly on the floor before death mercifully ended his suffering.

There was a bottle of whisky standing on the table, with a highball glass beside it. The glass held a small residue of brownish liquid. Off to one side was a small, round, squat bottle with the warning skull and cross-bones plainly imprinted on it. It was labeled *Strychnine*, and there was also the word *Poison* in large type.

Beside the bottle of strychnine were two torn pieces of notepaper that had been crumpled up and then smoothed and carefully placed one above the other, with torn edges in juxtaposition so that a superficial glance indicated that they were the torn top and bottom pieces of the same sheet of notepaper. A square box of the same notepaper and a ballpoint pen were on the extreme left-hand side of the table.

While Gentry and the two detectives knelt beside Marvin Dale's body, Shayne leaned over the table to read the scrawled handwriting on the sheet of torn notepaper:

Michael Shayne —
I will write this note while I can. I love my sister and have always forgiven her anything she did because I was too weak to protest, but I can't go on

any longer. She is a sweet girl and after seeing her with Charlin tonight I am revolted. Death holds no fear for me. John and Henrietta were old and mean and deserved to die. But this thing tonight is the last straw and I don't want to go on living.

Marvin Dale

Shayne read the torn note through without touching either half of it. Gentry got to his feet from beside the body with a sigh and said, "All the signs of typical strychnine poisoning. He's been dead for hours." He stood beside Shayne and looked down at the note, mumbling the words half aloud as he read them. Then he turned to the doorway and ordered the chauffeur curtly, "Come in here."

134

Charles walked in with his chin up and shoulders squared.

"Who are you?"

"Charles Morton. The chauffeur."

"What do you know about this?"

"He hasn't been touched," Charles said stolidly. "Nothing has been touched. . . ." He paused and his gaze flickered down to the table and the torn note. ". . . except that piece of paper. Mrs. Rogell discovered her brother's body about nine o'clock. The note was lying on the table . . . all in one piece. She called me in from my rooms over the garage and showed it to me. She wanted to tear it up before she called the police. I told her we couldn't destroy suicide evidence and tried to snatch it from her. It got torn and crumpled as you see it, but I insisted the police had to see it . . . no matter what interpretation you put on what Marvin said."

"Very co-operative and law-abiding of you," said Gentry harshly. He turned his gaze back to the torn paper and read aloud, " 'She is a sweet girl and after seeing her with Charles tonight I am utterly revolted.' How do you expect me to interpret that?"

"In the very nastiest way possible, I'm sure," said Charles steadily.

"How do you explain it?"

"Marvin was drunk last night. No drunker than usual, but . . . staggering. After I went out to the garage with a couple of pills Dr. Evans gave me, Mrs. Rogell became worried about my injuries and came out wearing her gown and robe just to be sure I needed no further medical attention. In his drunken state, Marvin saw her going out the back door and followed her up to my bedroom. He burst in on us and made a nasty scene . . . accusing his sister of all sorts of wild things. I

135

chased him out, and then sent Mrs. Rogell back to the house. That's why she wanted to destroy the note before anyone read it."

"Because it might be misinterpreted?" sneered Gentry. "Because other people might have the same idea about her presence in your bedroom late at night wearing a nightgown?"

Charles said, "People do have nasty minds."

"What does he mean by saying . . ." Gentry turned to look down and read again: " 'John and Henrietta were old and mean and deserved to die.' "

Charles said, "I don't know. That's for you to decide, isn't it? He didn't confide in me."

"Do you think it's a confession that he killed Rogell and tried to poison Henrietta?"

"I think that's for you to decide. Personally, I don't know that Mr. Rogell was killed or that anyone tried to poison Miss Henrietta."

"Where did the strychnine come from?"

"I think it's a bottle from the garage that the gardener keeps for killing moles. It looks exactly like one that was always kept in the garage, and I checked after I saw it, and that bottle is gone."

"Then you want us to believe that Marvin was so upset by surprising his sister in your bed that he got this bottle of poison from the garage, brought it in and wrote that note, and then drank a dose of it?"

"I don't particularly want you to believe anything," countered Charles doggedly. "There he is and there's the note. I convinced Mrs. Rogell that it would be better to give you the note and tell you the exact truth instead of destroying it as she wanted to do."

"Because then we might have suspected his death wasn't suicide?"

Charles said sullenly, "I didn't want to get mixed up in anything. There's already been too much loose talk around here by Miss Henrietta about poisoning and such. I had brains enough to realize that this . . . on top of all the other talk . . . would look mighty suspicious if he hadn't left any note. That's why I grabbed it away from her and wouldn't let her tear it up."

"What happened to your face . . . and your two front teeth?" demanded Gentry.

"Ask him." Charles jerked his head toward Shayne. "He entered the grounds illegally last night planning to dig up the body of Mrs. Rogell's pet dog, and he attacked me when I prevented him from doing it."

"That so, Mike?"

Shayne said, "I *attacked* him while he was holding a cocked, double-barreled shotgun on me. Marvin was pretty drunk that early in the evening while I was here, and he seemed determined to get a lot drunker. I don't see how he stayed sober enough to do this."

"He'd often drink so much he'd vomit it up and get sort of sober, and then start over," offered Charles.

There was the thin keening of a siren outside, and Gentry said, "That'll be the doc and the lab boys. Stay in here, Donovan. Petrie, you take this fellow downstairs and hold him. I want to talk to the servants and Mrs. Rogell."

Neither the maid nor Mrs. Blair were at all helpful. The maid had been out the preceding evening, returning to the house about midnight and going directly to her room beside Mrs. Blair's on the third floor without encountering anyone or being aware of any of the evening's happenings.

Mrs. Blair told them that as soon as Shayne and Dr. Evans had left the house, she insisted that Charles should get to bed, and had gone out with him to be sure he was comfortable and took the pills Dr. Evans had left.

When Shayne questioned her about the pills, she admitted she hadn't actually seen the chauffeur swallow them, but had seen him go into his bathroom holding them in his palm, had heard water running and seen him emerge without the pills.

Marvin had still been in the downstairs study with its well-stocked bar when she came in, and Mrs. Rogell was retiring when she locked the house and went up to her room. She had slept soundly, except for a telephone call from a policeman who demanded to speak to Charles —which demand she refused. Chief Gentry started to question her further about the call, but Shayne explained that he had made it. Mrs. Blair further stated that she knew nothing about anything that had gone on after she retired, that she had arisen at eight as was her custom and went directly to the kitchen to start preparing breakfast, where she had remained until Charles hurried in the back door and said that Mrs. Rogell had wakened him by his telephone extension to say that her brother had killed himself.

"We hurried up the stairs together," Mrs. Blair said, "and there was Mrs. Rogell in her nightclothes in the hall crying her eyes out. Charles and I both looked in Mr. Marvin's room and saw him lying on the floor and looking terrible. Then Charles closed the door and told me not to go in until the police came, and he went in Mrs. Rogell's sitting room with her still crying, and closed the door. I came back to the kitchen and wondered why you were so long getting here," she ended on a note of accusation.

Gentry asked, "When did you first see the body?"

"It was only a little after nine o'clock. Charles said he would call the police and I kept wondering why you didn't come."

Gentry said to Shayne, "It sounds as though he had a difficult time persuading her to give up the note." And he asked Mrs. Blair, "Did you see the bottle of poison on the table in Marvin's room?"

"That I did." She began to cry softly. "Strychnine. With the skull and crossbones plain to see. I told Charles it looked like the one the gardener keeps in the garage for killing moles in the garden and I always knew it was dangerous stuff to have around."

"When did you see it last?"

"Months, I guess. I don't have much occasion to go in the garage."

"Did everyone in the household know there was strychnine there?"

"I guess. It wasn't any secret," she said woefully.

Gentry shook his head soberly as they climbed the stairs to interview Anita Rogell. "I don't like any of this, Mike. There's a stink I can't get out of my nostrils." He stopped at the head of the stairs abruptly and suggested, "Let's see what Doc says before we talk to Mrs. Rogell."

Doc Higgins had completed his examination and he came out of the death room briskly as they turned toward it. He said, "A massive dose of strychnine . . . until I do a P.M. . . . taken in a highball about eight hours ago. Send him down to my charnelhouse as soon as you're through with him." He went on, and Chief Gentry went into the room to confer with his technicians, and Timothy Rourke sauntered out and rejoined Shayne. He grinned hopefully and said, "I'd like to get a statement from the stiff's sister giving her ideas on why he killed himself."

139

Shayne said, "We're going to talk to her now. Why don't you drift in behind us and stay in the background so Will can pretend he doesn't notice you? What do the boys say about the set-up in there?"

"Nothing much. He sat down and wrote that note about two o'clock, spiked a drink of good whisky with poison and drank it. Fingerprints all check. Everything's okay. Except that goddam suicide note. It doesn't *say* anything."

"They sure it's his handwriting . . . and the two torn pieces check?"

"They check perfectly. Couldn't possibly be faked. And George, the indentification man, found a lot of samples of Marvin's writing and swears it's the same . . . though the man was obviously pretty drunk when he wrote the note."

"He'd have to be to calmly swallow strychnine. Which is probably why the note isn't more rational. Very few suicide notes are wholly rational," Shayne went on with a frown, as though arguing a point with himself. "By the time they work themselves up to that point, they're not making too much sense. On the other hand, I've got a strange feeling about the wording of that note. . . ."

He broke off as Gentry came out and lumbered up the hall toward them. He said gruffly, "Let's go in and see how the lady of the house is holding up after the death of hubby *and* her brother."

Chapter fourteen

The door leading into Anita Rogell's upstairs sitting room was opened at Gentry's knock by the maid who had let them in downstairs. She held the door slightly open and turned her head to murmur, "It is the police, Madame," and then she opened it wider and stood aside for them to enter the room Lucy Hamilton had described to Shayne the preceding afternoon, and they walked into the same hothouse temperature Lucy had experienced.

Anita reclined on the chaise-longue across the room. She wore a violet silk dressing gown that was belted tightly about her slender waist, and she looked fragile and frightened and grief-stricken as she dabbed at her long-lashed eyes with a lacy handkerchief and her un-rouged lips quivered pathetically as she said, "Come in, gentlemen."

Will Gentry crossed the room and looked down at her. He said, "I'm sorry it's necessary to intrude at this time, Mrs. Rogell. I'm Chief Gentry of the Miami police, and I think you've met Mr. Shayne. He was in my office discussing the case with me this morning when the call came in about your brother, and I thought it well to bring him with me." He made no mention of Timothy Rourke who moved unobtrusively to one side in the background and gingerly seated himself on the edge of a slipper chair.

She said, "Yes. I . . . met Mr. Shayne briefly last evening. I believe he entered my property illegally with the avowed purpose of digging up my little dog who died recently."

Gentry didn't pursue that subject. He sat down in a chair a little to Anita's right, and Shayne seated himself on the other side of her. Gentry cleared his throat and his hand subconsciously strayed up to his inside coat pocket where he carried a supply of his stogies, and he half drew one out before sighing and replacing it in his pocket. He put both beefy palms flatly on his knees and said, "I'll be as brief as I can, Mrs. Rogell. I want you to tell me exactly what happened last night after Mr. Shayne and the doctor went away."

"Yes," she said in a low voice, dropping her long lashes and twining her fingers together nervously in her lap. "I . . . suppose I must. I'll try."

She drew in a deep breath and held it for a long time, and the tip of her tongue crept out to moisten her lips. Then she lifted her lashes and gazed at him appealingly and said in a little girl voice, "It's going to be most dreadfully difficult because I . . . you see . . . I realize that the foolish, impulsive thing I did was directly responsible for . . . for Marvin . . . for his . . ."

"Suicide," supplied Gentry bluntly. "I realize how guilty you must feel under the circumstances. Just tell us in your own way exactly what happened."

"Marvin was drinking," she said unhappily. "Mr. Shayne knows. He saw him briefly. After he and Dr. Evans went out the front, I went into the downstairs study and remonstrated with Marvin . . . begged him to stop drinking and go to bed as soon as he finished that drink. He was in an ugly mood and said he'd do

142

what he damn well pleased. I left him sitting there," she explained with dignity, "and came up to prepare for bed myself. I had a hot bath, and then I began thinking about Charles and started worrying about him. He has a great pride in his physical prowess and is so loyal and devoted to all of us that I knew he was terribly distressed by his encounter with Mr. Shayne. I was afraid . . . well . . . that he might start brooding about it and try to retaliate somehow, and I knew Dr. Evans had ordered him to take a strong sedative and go to sleep.

"I didn't realize, of course, that Mrs. Blair had much the same feeling and had already gone out with him and insisted that he take the pills and go right to bed, so I foolishly decided I would go out myself just to be sure he was all right. I slipped on a robe and went downstairs. There was still a light in the study, but I assumed Marvin was too stupid with drink to hear me going out."

She paused to bite her underlip thoughtfully. "I realize that makes it sound as though I felt guilty about going out to see Charles. I didn't . . . really. It was just that Marvin has a nasty mind, and once or twice before when he was drinking heavily he made some insinuating remarks about having a handsome and virile young chauffeur, and about . . . John being so much older than I. So I just wanted to avoid anything like that, and I went out the back way without knowing he heard me."

She paused again to run the tip of her tongue over her lips. "I saw the light was on in Charles's rooms over the garage, and I turned on the floodlight and went out. Charles came to the door in his pajamas and robe when I knocked, and he went back and got under the covers and I sat down for a minute after he told me he had already taken his pills and was waiting for them to take effect. He wanted to talk about Mr. Shayne and about how he'd been taken completely by surprise and hadn't a chance to defend himself when he was assaulted, and I tried to make him see it had come out all right because his vigilance *had* protected poor Daffy's grave. And that . . ." her voice faltered ". . . was all.

"But then Marvin came staggering and storming in and made the most awful scene." She bowed her head and covered her face with her hands for a moment, and Shayne thought wryly to himself that it was one of the most superb bits of acting he had ever witnessed on or off the stage. He glanced aside slyly at Gentry to see how he was reacting and wasn't surprised to see a look of fatherly compassion on the chief's heavy features. Because Gentry hadn't (he reminded himself) been present the past evening when she had stood against him and whispered, *"I want you, Michael Shayne."*

She took her hands away from her face and her eyes were wide and dewy and innocent. "He made the most awful and obscene accusations, and I had to get between him and the bed to prevent Charles from leaping up and tearing him limb from limb there and then."

She began sobbing quietly and covered her face again. "My own brother! I was so ashamed. And then suddenly I was furious." She lifted her head and her eyes sparkled and her chin was arrogant. "He had no right to even *think* such things. And I told him so. I threatened to scratch his eyes out if he didn't go at once, and he did go, but without apologizing or admitting he was wrong."

She drew a deep breath. "Well, I didn't know what to say except remind Charles that Marvin was drunk and wasn't responsible. And then I left in a few minutes and came back in to bed and I didn't see Marvin again until . . . until this morning when I . . . when I went to his room. . . ." She bowed her head and sobbed again.

144

Very gravely and sympathetically, Will Gentry said, "I know it's difficult, Mrs. Rogell, but I want you to tell me exactly how it happened and what you found."

"Yes . . . well . . . I awoke about nine o'clock and all I could think about was what had happened last night. After Marvin sobered up I was sure he would realize what an awful thing he had done, and I went to his room determined that he should apologize to me and to Charles. I knocked on his door and opened it when he didn't reply . . . thinking he was still sleeping it off. And the light was on and . . . there he lay. On the floor. And there was the bottle of strychnine on the table. I knew he was dead. I knew it even before I forced myself to kneel down and touch his cold flesh. And then I looked around wildly and saw . . . the note he had written and left lying on the table beside his glass.

"I read it half a dozen times, I guess, trying to understand it . . . to understand *why* he had taken his own life. Then I realized how it sounded . . . how it would look to some outsider like . . . well, like you. The police. So I snatched it up and ran back to my room."

She shuddered at the recollection. "I know I shouldn't have touched it. Charles said I should have left it lying right where it was. But I was hysterical and I didn't think. I didn't think anything except trying to keep anyone from knowing why my brother had taken his own life. Because he was ashamed of his sister. Because he thought I was a loose and wanton female . . . being intimate with another man before my husband was even in his grave.

"So I called Charles on his extension and told him. And he ran into the house and told Mrs. Blair and they went to Marvin's room, and then Charles came in, terribly worried because Marvin hadn't left any suicide note. He said the police were *always* suspicious if they didn't find a note . . . and that with Henrietta's crazy accusations against me they would probably suspect I had put the strychnine in Marvin's drink too.

"I wasn't even going to show him the note until he made me understand how really serious it might be. Then I read it to him and told him I'd rather tear it up and *be* suspected than have it all come out in the papers that my brother had killed himself because he was ashamed of me. And I did start to tear it up in front of Charles, but he snatched at it and tore the top part off, and then he pried my hand open and got the bottom part and said we *had* to give the two parts to the police.

"And he said you always kept the contents of suicide notes a secret and wouldn't give the text out to any papers if they had something in them that embarrassed living people, and I finally agreed. And you won't, will you?" she ended pleadingly. "Let it be printed in the papers, I mean. Even though Marvin was mistaken and I can prove there's nothing like that between Charles and me, you know how they'd crucify me. And everyone who read it in the papers would believe the worst. People always do."

"Why, no, ma'am," Gentry assured her in a kindly voice. "In cases like this we don't give out such information to reporters."

From his side pocket he withdrew Marvin's note which had been carefully put together with scotch tape so that the ragged edges of the two portions fitted against each other exactly.

"Now this first part," he said slowly. "Your story and the one Charles told seems to explain that all right. But what did he mean by saying: 'Death holds no fears for me.' And: 'John and Henrietta were old and mean and deserved to die.' Is that a confession that he killed your husband and tried to poison Henrietta?"

"I just don't know what it means," she confessed tearfully. "Charles and I went over and over it together, but it just sounds crazy to me. I can't believe that's what it means. I just can't. Marvin couldn't kill anybody. He just wasn't like that. He was . . . well, he was weak and lazy, and he drank too much. And he knew John didn't like him hanging around here and borrowing money from me, but Marvin would never have done anything like that. Besides, John died from a heart attack. I was there and saw it happen. And Dr. Evans said there wasn't the slightest question about it. So I simply don't know what Marvin meant when he wrote that line. He was drunk, of course, and terribly upset by what he believed about Charles and me."

"I realize that," Gentry soothed her. "Just while we're on the subject, let's go back to your husband's death. I understand Mr. Peabody was upstairs with him going over some business affairs from about ten until midnight. Where were you and Marvin?"

"Downstairs in the study. I was reading a magazine and Marvin was drinking . . . as usual. I went up a few minutes before twelve to take John his hot milk and give him his medicine in it."

"Digitalis, wasn't it?" Gentry encouraged her.

"Tincture of digitalis. He's been taking twelve drops in hot chocolate milk for years for his heart condition."

"Tell me exactly what you did that night. Was there anything different from any other night?"

"N-o-o. That is, Mr. Peabody wasn't always sitting with him, of course. I got the thermos from the dining table where Mrs. Blair always left it, and came up through this room and into the connecting bathroom where I picked up the medicine bottle. And I went in John's room where he and Mr. Peabody had finished

147

their business and were chatting, and set the cup and thermos beside John's bed and measured out twelve drops in the cup.

"Then I told Mr. Peabody he'd have to go, and he told John good night and I filled the cup and John drank it."

"Did you realize how important it was to measure the dose carefully?"

"Oh, yes. Exactly twelve drops and not a single one more. That's why I insisted I should always do it myself, because Dr. Evans said even one or two extra drops might be bad for John, his heart being like it was."

"All right. He drank the milk straight down?"

"Well, it was pretty hot, and I guess he took a sip or two until it got cool enough to drink it down in a couple of gulps."

"So it was a few minutes after Peabody left that he actually drank it?"

"Not more than five minutes, I'm sure."

"What did you do then?"

"Well, he settled back in bed and I stayed to . . . talk to him until he dropped off to sleep. He liked me to do that."

"Did you . . . kiss him good night or anything like that?"

She lowered her eyelids a moment and clenched her hands tightly together in her lap, and then demanded angrily, "Why do you beat around the bush about it? I'm a grownup married woman. Those two detectives you sent out kept prying around the same way. You want to know whether we had sexual relations, don't you? Because that old fool of Dr. Jenson had the nerve to warn him that he shouldn't marry a younger woman for fear his heart might give out in the excitement of the sex act. Well, we *didn't* that night," she spat out. "In that way it was different from most nights. He did begin

148

loving me up, if you must know, and I thought he wanted me to get in bed with him, but then suddenly he kind of stiffened and began breathing fast and I got frightened and . . . and that was it."

"All right," said Gentry stolidly. "Thank you for being frank with me." He got to his feet. "Are you going ahead with your husband's funeral as planned?"

"I think so. If you don't object."

"Why should I object?"

"Charles thought . . . well, he said that maybe after you read Marvin's note you would think that was a reason for ordering an autopsy on John. But I told him you couldn't do it if I didn't give my consent, and I'd never in the world do that."

"Why, no," said Gentry. "Go right ahead with the funeral if you want. I have no objection whatsoever. But you understand that an autopsy on your brother will be mandatory. The law requires it in a case like his."

She said listlessly, "I understand about that and I guess I can't stop you. Although I do think it's utterly barbarous and indecent."

Gentry said, "I'm sorry," and the three men left the room together.

Chapter fifteen

Marvin Dale's body had been taken away, and Detective Donovan had gone downstairs to join Petrie and the chauffeur in the study. They found the city detectives seated in chairs near the door, with Charles sullenly lounging in a deep chair at the other side of the room.

Gentry strode in flatfootedly and crossed to stop directly in front of the chauffeur. He deliberately extracted a black cigar from his inner pocket, bit off the end and spat it on the floor, struck a match and held it to the other end, inhaled deeply and thrust his blunt jaw out. His features and his voice were granite-hard as he said, "Don't get the idea I'm buying any of this, Morton. I've got a pretty good notion about the sort of games you've been playing with your employer's child-bride behind his back, and I think it's just too bad that her pants got so hot last night that she couldn't let you go to bed alone. But your sex life is no concern of mine except as it has a bearing on murder."

Charles said, "Marvin committed suicide, if that's what you're talking about."

"Did he?"

The chauffeur shrugged stolidly. "I didn't see him drink the poison, if that's what you mean."

"It's too bad somebody didn't," grated Gentry. "Because I'm telling you right now I don't picture Marvin Dale as the sort of moral character who'd be so shocked to discover his sister's infidelity that he'd sit down and swallow strychnine. Nor do I believe for one moment that he hasn't known all along what you and Mrs. Rogell were up to."

"Why tell all this to me?" flared Charles.

"Because I want you to know you're still in trouble, and this investigation isn't closed by a long shot. Don't try to leave town." The police chief turned on his heel and strode toward the door, jerking his head at Petrie and Donovan to follow him.

Shayne went out in the hall behind him with Rourke, and told the reporter, "Why don't you ride back with Will, and write your story on Marvin? I'll be along later."

Rourke grinned amiably. "Going to stick around and chaperon the widow?"

"Something like that." Shayne watched them go out the front door, and then went back to the kitchen where he found Mrs. Blair seated at the table drinking a cup of coffee.

She offered him one and he thanked her and told her he would drink it black, and sat down opposite her with a cigarette, and asked, "Did you see the suicide note Marvin left?"

She shook her head. "Nobody showed it to me."

"Just how flagrant were Charles and Mrs. Rogell about their affair before her husband's death?"

She compressed her lips firmly and met his gaze across the table. "It's not for me to gossip about people in the house where I work."

"You won't be working here long," Shayne said flatly. "You certainly know that John Rogell left you fifty thousand dollars in his will."

"I know he told me he was going to."

"Why?"

"Why not?" she returned with spirit. "He had plenty and we've been friends a long, long time."

Shayne said, "Friends?"

"Maybe you don't know that he and Miss Henrietta roomed at my boarding house in Central City, Colorado, when he was just a prospector."

"I know all about that. And how he came back there after your husband died and brought you here to be his housekeeper . . . and installed you in the adjoining suite until he married Anita and you had to move up to the third floor. And now he's left you a fortune. Were all of those just friendly gestures?"

She said without rancor, "You've been listening to Henrietta. She's got a nasty mind and always has hated me since she went to law against John and I got on the witness stand and told the plain truth about how generous he was to her."

"Are you denying that you and Mr. Rogell were more than just friends?"

"I shan't waste my breath denying it," she said with simple dignity. "I don't think you've any right to sit in my kitchen and say such things with the funeral not more than an hour away."

Shayne said, "Wouldn't you want to see his murderer caught . . . if he was murdered as Henrietta thinks?"

"If he *was* murdered," she said with emphasis. "But I never have believed that one minute. Who'd have a reason?"

"Suppose he had become suspicious of Anita and Charles?"

"I swear he never was. He thought the sun rose and set in that girl. And I must say she made him a real good wife."

152

"Do you know that Marvin is supposed to have taken poison because he surprised her out in Charles's bedroom last night?"

"I didn't know that, but he was probably so larruping drunk he might've done anything."

Shayne asked, "Do you think Marvin might have killed Rogell?"

"Why would he? He had it mighty soft here."

"But Rogell didn't like the way he sponged off Anita. With him out of the way, he'd have it a lot softer."

"Then why would he go and kill himself a couple days later?"

"That," said Shayne morosely, "is one of several questions that bothers me. I wish you'd remember back to the night Rogell died. I understand you were in the kitchen until about eleven o'clock, and went up to bed after heating his milk and putting it in the thermos jug."

"Like I did every night in the world. Before he got married I used to measure out his medicine in the cup myself, and when *she* came she did it."

Shayne looked around the surgically clean, white kitchen speculatively. "Think back to that night," he urged her. "Let's theorize that someone did add something to his drink that caused his death. Who *could* have done it . . . had the physical opportunity?"

"I had the best chance."

Shayne said, "I know. Who else?"

"Well, Charles was in here while I was washing out the thermos with hot water and heating the milk to go in it. I remember because I had to stop him from drinking the last glass of milk there was left in the refrigerator. I remember because it was just a lucky chance I caught him in time. I would have sworn there was another bottle left after dinner, but there wasn't. And I scolded

153

Charles for not checking careful before he poured his glass out because he *knew* Mr. Rogell always had to have a cup at night. Everybody in the house knew they mustn't ever drink the last cup until I'd fixed his thermos."

"Then he actually had it poured out before you noticed?"

"Yes, he did. He had a plate of cookies here on the table and I was washing out the thermos at the sink."

"Then if he knew it was the last glass, he could have put something in it and then stalled around before drinking it so you'd notice and take it away from him?"

"He could have done that," she agreed doubtfully. "But I didn't notice him stalling any. He was about to take a sip when I saw it was the last in the bottle and snatched it out of his hand."

"So that gives us Charles," Shayne said with satisfaction. "After you left the filled thermos on the dining table, what then?"

"I went upstairs. I think Anita and her brother were in the study. Henrietta came out of her door and met me in the hall and reminded me I was going to lend her a book I had from the library. She went up with me to the third floor and sat and visited in my room until we heard Mrs. Rogell screaming that John was taken sick. We both ran down together and Marvin and Mr. Peabody came up from downstairs."

"Did Henrietta leave your room at all during that hour?"

"No. We just sat and talked."

"And the thermos jug was downstairs all the time. You wouldn't have heard anybody going up or down the stairs during that time?"

"I didn't, and I don't think I could've."

154

"While you were in your room with Henrietta, was your door open or closed?"

She considered this thoughtfully, compressing her lips and blinking her eyelids. "The door was shut. I'm sure it was. I can *see* Henrietta coming in behind me and closing it."

"So you were really shut off from the second floor and the other people in the house."

"That's right." She regarded him steadily across the kitchen table.

"This medicine of Mr. Rogell's that has been mentioned so often. Tincture of digitalis. Did he always take exactly the same amount?"

"Twelve drops out of a medicine dropper," she replied promptly. "For two or three years now."

"And everyone in the house knew about it? Where it was kept in the bathroom?"

"In the medicine cabinet there. It surely wasn't any secret."

"And was it common knowledge that an overdose would be dangerous?"

"It certainly was."

"Do *you* know exactly what effect a large overdose might have had?"

Mrs. Blair hesitated a long moment before replying, giving the impression that she was trying hard and honestly to give a correct reply.

"I think I remember . . . I'm pretty sure I do now . . . that when Dr. Evans took over the case he gave us a lecture about it. About how careful we must be in measuring it out. That even a double dose might bring on a heart attack that would take him off." An acid note crept into her voice as she added, "That's when his wife said *she'd* see to it that he got his medicine every

155

night . . . intimating that *I* wasn't to be trusted any more to measure it careful enough."

"Then all of you knew that an overdose might cause him to die . . . exactly as he did die," pressed Shayne.

"Are you saying that's what did happen, Mr. Shayne?" There was outraged horror in the housekeeper's voice.

"I'm not saying anything. I'm pointing out that if someone in the house did want Rogell to die . . . and hoped it would appear a natural death . . . that the means was ready to his hand."

"*Did* somebody put extra digitalis in his milk that night?"

Shayne shrugged. "If they did, Dr. Evans can't be blamed for believing it was a natural death. And I understand the widow has refused to allow an autopsy which might have proved different."

"I see what you're driving at." Mrs. Blair's voice was grim. "And I stood up for her when she said she couldn't stand having John's body cut up like a dog or a rat in a laboratory. I felt just the same way. But now I wonder."

Shayne said, "All we can do at this point is to wonder, Mrs. Blair. Let's jump, now, to the evening when Daffy died."

"What about it?" She settled herself heavily in an attitude that indicated she was prepared to defend herself against accusations.

Shayne said, "Harold Peabody was here for dinner."

She nodded. "First time since Mr. Rogell died."

"Who planned the dinner menu that night?"

"I did," she told him defiantly. "Mrs. Rogell didn't bother very often with things like that."

"Then it was wholly your own idea to have a separate dish of creamed chicken for Henrietta?"

"What's wrong in that? The others were having shrimp casserole and any kind of seafood made her deathly sick."

"Nothing wrong with it in principle. I suppose everyone present knew of her allergy, and that there would be a special dish for her?"

"They did if they had ears to hear by. Always harping on it, she was."

"And there were two separate chafing dishes on the sideboard from which you served dinner?"

"A chafing dish of creamed chicken, and the covered casserole on an electric warming plate."

"Sitting there how long before dinner was served?"

"The chafing dish for maybe twenty minutes. I made the chicken in that, and gave it a stir now and then while I set the table."

"I understand that Mr. Rogell's death was discussed before dinner."

"There was hell to pay," said Mrs. Blair succinctly. "Henrietta raving about how she knew John had been murdered and she was going to prove it if she had to go to the governor of the state of Florida to get an autopsy on John before he was cremated. And all the others trying to shush her, and her ranting louder than ever the more they shushed."

"Suppose someone had decided to put strychnine in her chicken," said Shayne quietly. "Who had the opportunity?"

"Any one of them. They were milling around in the dining room with drinks in their hands . . . all talking to Henrietta at once."

"Including Charles?"

"Oh, no. He was here in the kitchen while that was going on."

157

"Then we can eliminate Charles if something was put into her chicken?"

"Well, I . . . I don't know as I'd say that. He's always good about helping at the table beforehand. Like putting ice in the glasses and pouring water. He might have been in and out once or twice."

"Did you see Henrietta give the dog a saucer of her chicken?"

"I certainly did not," sniffed Mrs. Blair. "For my money, I don't believe she ever did it. I think it was just something that came to her when the poor little thing got sick like she did. Accusing me of serving her with poisoned food!"

"Who suggested that you dispose of the remaining chicken and wash out the dishes before the detectives got here?"

"Nobody. I was that upset and mad when she started screaming her chicken was poisoned that I snatched up the plate and dish and carried them out and dumped them." She glared at him angrily. "Make something out of that if you want to. Like those other detectives tried to. But suppose you'd been cooking for other folks for thirty years and suddenly got accused of putting poison in a dish. Wouldn't you be mad and upset?"

"I probably would," Shayne soothed her. "If someone around this house wanted strychnine, Mrs. Blair, where would he go for it?"

"The same place Marvin went last night, I guess. Right out in the garage where the gardener kept it for moles."

"And I suppose everyone here knew about *that*, too," sighed Shayne.

"Except maybe Mr. Peabody. And I wouldn't have been sure Marvin knew either because he was generally

158

so soaked in alcohol he didn't know much that was going on right around him."

Mrs. Blair glanced up at the electric clock on the wall behind him and gasped, "Mercy me! I only got twenty minutes to get ready for the funeral."

Shayne left the kitchen and was striding down the wide hallway toward the front door when he heard his name spoken faintly and hesitantly from behind him. He turned and saw Anita posed on the winding stairway, about halfway down. A black-gloved hand rested lightly on the railing, and she wore a simple black suit unrelieved by any ornaments or jewelry whatsoever. She had very little make-up on, and beneath a black, velvet beret her golden-silk hair was tucked in carefully, giving her a wanly appealing little-girl look.

Shayne stood in the hallway and watched her come down the rest of the stairs. She glided sedately from one step to the next, as befitted a grieving widow on the way to her husband's funeral—and a woman whose brother had just committed suicide, Shayne reminded himself cynically, because he believed her to be unchaste.

Anita came close to him, her head tilted slightly, lips parted wistfully. "I wanted to see you again, Michael. I couldn't let you go away thinking . . ." She paused and demurely lowered her lashes. A faint breath of her perfume came into his nostrils and her parted lips were no more than a foot from his. ". . . the same awful things about me that Marvin thought," she hurried on breathlessly. "You don't, do you?"

He said, "Does it matter what I think, Anita? I assure you I wouldn't go off and swallow strychnine if I did."

A little stricken cry issued from her lips, and she swayed toward him, keeping her eyes closed.

159

"It does matter. Terribly. I couldn't stand to think that after . . . after what happened between us last night I could have deliberately gone out to Charles and . . . and . . ."

Shayne laughed.

She jerked erect and her eyelids flew open and he saw naked hate in the depths of her glorious eyes.

"How can you stand there and sneer at me?"

Shayne said brutally, "It's easy, Anita. Simplest thing in the world. All I have to do is think about how your husband died . . . and then a little dog . . . and Marvin."

He turned on his heel and went to the front door without looking back.

Chapter sixteen

Getting off the elevator, Michael Shayne strode across the hall and mechanically reached for the knob of the door lettered:

MICHAEL SHAYNE
Investigations

The knob turned but the door refused to open. He cursed himself methodically and in a low voice because he had forgotten momentarily that Lucy Hamilton would not be inside the office waiting for him, and he unlocked the door and flung it open with savage force.

The small anteroom was empty and silent. Lucy's chair in front of the typewriter desk beyond the low railing was empty, and the silence was oppressive.

There were deep trenches in Shayne's cheeks and his jaws were set together tightly as he turned away after one fleeting glance at Lucy's desk and walked through the door into his private office. He circled the big desk to a filing cabinet against the wall, pulled out a drawer on its ball-bearings and lifted a half-full bottle of cognac from it. He thumped the bottle down on the desk in front of his swivel chair, turned to a water cabinet and got down two paper cups which he fitted one inside the other. He filled the inner cup to the brim with amber liquid from the bottle and settled his rangy figure into the swivel chair. With a lighted cigarette dangling between the first two fingers of his left hand, he took a long drink of brandy and closed his eyes.

Distorted images danced before his eyes as he fought to concentrate on the problem at hand. Lucy Hamilton seated at her desk in the outer room. Henrietta Rogell in her mannish bathrobe last night pouring a heavy slug of whisky into her glass. Lucy seated across from him at a white-clothed table, her brown eyes dancing with life and gaiety as she lifted a champagne glass to her lips. Anita Rogell standing against him last night and her warmly timbred voice telling him wantonly, *"I want you, Michael Shayne."* Lucy Hamilton seated sedately at one end of the sofa in her own apartment with bottles and glasses on the low coffee table in front of her, shaking the brown curls back from her animated face while she leaned forward to pour him a final good night drink before shooing him out so she could go to bed. The stiffened body of a tiny Pekinese that appeared to be grinning at him. Lucy Hamilton . . .

Shayne jerked his eyes open angrily and glared across the silent office. His right hand instinctively strayed out to grasp the nested paper cups, and he had them halfway to his mouth when he grated, "Goddam it to hell!" and set them down again without drinking.

Thus far he had done nothing about Lucy. Nothing at all. He was relying on the kidnaper to keep her alive as a hostage until the remains of John Rogell were consumed by fire and his murderer was positive that all evidence of murder had been consumed with the body.

After that—what?

Michael Shayne didn't know.

He was no closer to a solution now than he had been

when Henrietta first came to him more than twenty-four hours ago.

Marvin Dale? There was his suicide and the ambiguous note he had left behind. But if Marvin Dale had put the digitalis in Rogell's milk—what about Lucy? Was it conceivable that Dale had snatched her and hidden her away, and then swallowed strychnine without mentioning a word about her in his farewell note?

No! Shayne told himself savagely. It wasn't conceivable. Yet only Rogell's killer would have a motive for snatching Lucy.

So Dale wasn't the murderer.

Yet the man *had* committed suicide.

Or had he?

Michael Shayne sat at his desk tensely, his eyes narrowed and burning across the room while he pondered every word and phrase of the suicide note which he had memorized. Somewhere, somehow, there was a clue in those scribbled words that eluded him. The answer was there. Some tiny portion of his subconscious mind had glimpsed that fact when he first read the words, but it refused to come through to him.

He growled another oath deep in his throat and forced himself to relax. To cease concentrating. To stop trying to force it out of his subconscious. If he could divert his thoughts into other channels—blank his mind away from the problem entirely—

He stretched out his arm and lifted the telephone and dialed Chief Will Gentry's private number at police headquarters.

When Gentry answered, he asked briskly, "Any long-distance calls for me, Will? From Colorado particularly?"

"Your man called here a little before twelve. He got

163

hold of nothing positive in Central City except ancient gossip and strong suspicions among the townfolk that John Rogell and Betty Blair did have an affair in the old days. It was revived when he hired her to come to Miami as his housekeeper, and the town is buzzing again now that he's left her that hunk of cash in his will. One other small thing, Mike. A lot of old-timers agree that Henrietta was the aggressive strong one in the early days, and that it was her vigor and drive that laid the groundwork for the Rogell fortune."

"Not much there that we didn't already know or suspect," grumbled Shayne. "Anything else?"

"Nothing important. A preliminary report indicates that Dale swallowed a big batch of strychnine on top of one hell of a lot of liquor some time between midnight and dawn."

"What do you make of the suicide note?"

"It bothers me. But, goddam it, Mike, it's undoubtedly genuine. It's been examined microscopically by our expert. Same pen as was lying there, same notepaper. Handwriting is positively Dale's, indicating great mental stress and probable alcoholic haze at the time of writing. Exactly what you would expect under the circumstances. What are you doing about Lucy?" Gentry ended abruptly.

"Funeral going off all right?" countered the redhead.

"So far as I know. I've got four men covering it and they haven't reported anything. Goddam it, Mike! I think it's time we stepped in. If Lucy is . . ."

"You promised me until three o'clock." Beads of sweat had formed on Shayne's forehead and were coursing down the trenches in his cheeks.

"I know I did, you stubborn Mick. But I don't see . . ."

"I don't either," Shayne interrupted him much more

164

calmly than he felt. "I'm coming over, Will. I can't just sit here . . ."

He dropped the receiver and slowly got to his feet. His glance fell on the half-filled cup on his desk and he reached for it, checked his big hand before he touched it and hesitated a long moment.

Then his lips came back from his teeth in a terrifying sort of grin, and he swept up the twin cups and downed the liquor in two gulps. He was getting childish, by God. Or senile, maybe. Any time Mike Shayne walked out of his office and left a half-finished drink on his desk it would be time for him to turn in his license.

And maybe it was at that.

But not quite yet. Not until three o'clock.

Not until he was convinced that Lucy—

Chapter seventeen

Chief Will Gentry was seated alone at his desk stolidly munching on a ham sandwich and sipping from a container of black coffee when the detective walked in. There were some typewritten sheets shoved back carelessly in front of him, and beside his right hand lay Marvin Dale's suicide note. Back from that was the box of notepaper and the ballpoint pen with which the note had been written.

Gentry looked up from studying the note with an impatient shrug of his broad shoulders. "Can't keep my eyes off this thing," he muttered. "Keep reading it over and over with the feeling it's trying to say *something* to me that I don't get."

Shayne nodded, hooking his toe under the rung of a straight chair and dragging it close to the side of the chief's desk. "I know. It's a hunch that won't break through." He closed his eyes and recited the contents of the note, spacing the words carefully and avoiding giving any one of them special emphasis:

"I will write this note while I can. I love my sister and have always forgiven her anything she did because I was too weak to protest, but I can't go on any longer. She is a sweet girl and after seeing her with Charles tonight I am revolted. Death holds no fears for me. John and Henrietta were old and mean and deserved to die. But this thing tonight is the last straw and I don't want to go on living. Marvin Dale."

He stopped speaking and the words hung in the silent air between the two men. Gentry took a gulp of coffee and wiped his thick lips with the back of his hand.

"Boil it right down, Mike, it doesn't *say* anything. You keep thinking it must make sense and each sentence seems like it does, but when you add it up . . . what you got?"

Shayne said somberly, "A drunken rigmarole."

"Sure, the guy was tight. But, like I say, you take each single sentence and it doesn't sound so drunk. It's when you put them all together. . . ." Gentry wolfed the last bite of his lunch and spread out beefy hands in a helpless gesture.

Shayne said, "I know." He lit a cigarette and leaned forward, narrowing his eyes at the note, the torn halves placed in perfect juxtaposition and fastened with scotch tape. His right hand reached out and toyed with the octagonal ballpoint pen which the experts declared had written the note. "No fingerprints on this thing, I suppose."

"You know better'n that, Mike. Sure, there was a whorl or two. But what the hell? You know all the chemical tests they got. That pen wrote the note . . . and it's Marvin Dale's handwriting."

"On a sheet of paper out of this box." Shayne idly lifted a sheet between thumb and forefinger and weighed it thoughtfully. It was thick, and somewhat creamy in color, a single unfolded sheet about five by eight inches in size, obviously expensive, but with no monogram or engraved heading.

He stared at it for a long time, with blue smoke curling up from the tip of his cigarette past his narrowed eyes. A curiously blank expression spread over his rugged features, much as though a sort of self-hypnosis gripped him, and then very carefully, very deliberately, he placed the blank sheet of paper exactly beside the mended note, meticulously lining up the two sides so they touched, and putting the top edges in perfect alignment.

In an absolutely flat voice, he said, "Got it, Will. We should both have our heads examined."

"What you got?" Gentry craned his neck to look.

Shayne's forefinger stabbed down decisively to the bottom edges of the two sheets, mutely pointing out the fact that the sheet on which the note was written was a good quarter inch shorter than the unused sheet he had placed beside it.

"But they can't be different!" exploded Gentry. "Same watermark and same thickness and color. They ran all sorts of tests. . . ."

"But not the same size sheet," Shayne pointed out. "That's the one simple test your experts didn't think about making, Will."

"Even if it didn't come from that same box, I don't see what it gets us," grumbled Gentry. "It's still in Dale's handwriting, and so . . ."

"I think I know exactly where it gets us." Shayne's voice was harsh with assurance. "Don't you get it yet? It *is* the same paper, but . . . when the torn halves were pasted back together it doesn't come out the same length."

"You mean there's one line missing out of the middle? One line that might change the whole meaning, if it was there? Yeah, but . . . but . . . Wait, Mike, goddam it! That can't be right either. Those rough edges absolutely coincide. Even under a microscope. If they'd been torn twice in order to eliminate one line, they couldn't still match up."

Shayne said quietly, "Watch this, Will." He took two fresh sheets from the box and lined them up meticulously on the desk so one lay exactly on top of the other. Then he gently moved the top sheet down a quarter of an inch, keeping the edges in alignment. Placing the palm of his left hand solidly across the lower portion of the two sheets so neither one could move, he took hold of the double edge between right thumb and forefinger and ripped the two sheets across just above the side of his hand.

Then he discarded the lower half of the top sheet and put it aside with the upper half of the bottom sheet. He asked, "Got any scotch tape?" and fitted the upper half of the top sheet exactly together with the torn edge of the lower half of the bottom sheet.

Gentry jerked open a drawer and got out a spool of tape, ripped off a small piece and fastened the two halves of the different sheets together while Shayne held them carefully.

Shayne said grimly, "There we are. Two torn halves that fit together so perfectly that a microscope couldn't detect anything. But just about a quarter inch shorter than the original size."

"The top and bottom parts of two different notes . . . torn across like you did so they match. But how in hell did the wording ever match up?" Gentry shifted his gaze to the note. "The top part doesn't even end with a period. The sentence goes right on to the next part."

"Looking just as though it was intended to be that way," agreed Shayne. "That must have been pure coincidence. One that somebody noticed and was smart

169

enough to take advantage of after he read both notes and realized the two parts could be made to sound like the same one, if no one suspected differently."

"Why two notes? Both in Dale's handwriting . . . ?"

Shayne shrugged. "Two drafts of the same note, maybe. The guy was drunk and under a lot of stress. Maybe he had some reason to write two notes. The second one might even have been addressed to someone else."

"Then we'll never know what they really said when placed in the right order."

"Maybe not. But we do know damned well that both Charles and Anita were lying when they told us how the note got torn." Shayne glanced at his watch, his eyes glittering with excitement. "That funeral ought to be about over. I want to be out there at the house when they get back." He drummed the tips of his fingers on the desk, thinking hard. "Have you got Harold Peabody's office number?"

"It's here some place in some notes." Gentry scrabbled among the papers, found a list of names and addresses and read off the number to Shayne.

The detective dialed it, and when a woman's voice answered, he asked for Mr. Peabody.

"I'm sorry he isn't in just now. Could someone else be of help?"

Shayne said, "No. It's a personal matter. When do you expect him?"

"Well, he's attending a funeral, and I'm not sure . . ."

"Rogell. Of course," said Shayne heartily. "Do you know what Harold planned to do afterward?"

"Why, yes." The voice was noticeably warmer. "I believe he planned to go straight on out with Mrs. Rogell to hear the will read."

Shayne breathed, "Thanks, honey," and hung up. He leaped to his feet and told Gentry, "Have Petrie and Donovan meet me at Rogell's fast as they can make it." He snatched up the note addressed to him, shoved it in his pocket, and went out of the office fast.

Chapter eighteen

There were three cars parked in front of the house when Shayne swung into the driveway. He pulled up behind them and leaped out, heard screaming rubber at the estate entrance and turned his head to see Petrie and Donovan on his heels in a radio cruiser.

He lifted one hand in greeting and hurried up the steps and across the porch. The two city detectives came panting up behind him as he put his finger on the electric button and held it there.

"What's up, Mike?" demanded Donovan. "We got a flash from the chief . . ."

The door opened and Shayne jerked out, "Come in and clam up." He shoved forward past the frightened and protesting maid, and they tramped in close behind him.

There were voices coming from the study beyond the archway on the right, and they ceased abruptly as Shayne entered through the open portières with the two policemen on his heels. He stopped just inside the archway and surveyed the small gathering with bleak eyes.

They were all there to hear John Rogell's will read, he noted with satisfaction. Anita and Charles and Henrietta and Mrs. Blair. And Harold Peabody hovering behind Anita's chair, and an elderly man who was a

172

stranger to him, seated apart from the others with a legal-sized folder of papers bound in blue cardboard open on his knees.

They all stared at him in silence and in varying degrees of surprise, apprehension and defiance as he looked from one face to another.

Harold Peabody spoke first. He straightened his body into a sort of strut behind Anita's chair, and spoke acidly, "This is a private conference, Mr. Shayne."

"And I'm a private detective," growled the redhead. He looked toward the elderly man who was obviously a lawyer and said, "Sorry to interrupt your proceedings, but I don't think this will take very long." He advanced toward Anita who shrank back from him in the depths of a big chair and looked small and defenseless, and stood towering over her as he said mercilessly, "I want the truth about this note signed by your brother's name." His hand came out of his pocket holding the crumpled note and he waved it in front of her face.

"I know you lied about it," he told her conversationally. "I know you didn't find it lying beside his body as you said, and I know it didn't get torn in half the way you told me it did. Hell," he went on in a tone of utter disgust, "it's perfectly evident that this is two halves of two different notes. The only thing I *don't* know is what each note said when put together correctly, but I've got a damned good idea that both of them contained evidence that you murdered your husband, and that's why you got Charles to lie for you to help you pass this off as a real note."

"Don't answer him, Anita." The chauffeur was on his feet instantly, his voice thick with rage. "He's trying to trick you. He don't know . . ."

Shayne didn't glance aside. He said sharply, "Shut him up, Donovan."

173

The big detective moved behind him swiftly with drawn revolver and Shayne continued to stand over Anita with his eyes boring into hers.

"If the original notes didn't say that, you'd better tell us what they *did* say. You've covered up for Charles as far as you can," he went on remorselessly. "Now you'd better start thinking about your own neck. Or maybe it's too late for that. Was it *you* who killed your own brother after you realized you could fix a note so it'd look like suicide?"

"No, no!" she cried in a strangled voice. "It was Charles. He told me . . ."

She was interrupted by a shout from Charles, a muttered oath from Donovan and the solid clunk of a revolver barrel against flesh and bone. This was followed by the heavy thump of a solid body against the floor, and Shayne turned his head to see Donovan kneeling over Charles's recumbent figure and snapping handcuffs on the man's lax wrists.

Shayne turned back to the widow dispassionately. "He won't make any further trouble. Tell us what happened."

"I want to," she sobbed. "I wanted to all the time, but he frightened me. He showed me Marvin's two notes and they did sound like he thought I'd killed John and tried to poison Henrietta. And he showed me how it'd work if we tore them apart in just the right place and put the two wrong halves together. And we made up that story about Marvin catching us together in his room so the note would make sense that way. And Marvin was already dead," she wept on, hanging her head piteously. "I guess I really knew Charles had done it after frightening him into writing those two notes, but I was so scared and upset after what happened to Daffy and all that I hardly knew what I was doing."

174

"You say there were two notes originally. Addressed to whom?"

"One was written to you and one to me," she told him faintly. "He meant to hide them some place in the hope that one of them would be found, I guess."

"But Charles got hold of them before he had a chance to hide them?" put in Shayne harshly.

"Yes. I guess so."

"What did the original notes say?"

"I remember every word of the one written to me." Anita shuddered and hung her head.

"What did he say?"

"He started out: 'Dear Sis'." She lifted her chin and recited tonelessly, " 'If Charles kills me tonight as I expect him to, I hope this note or one I'm writing to Mike Shayne and hiding in a different place will be found. I kept quiet after I suspected you and Charles of murdering your husband, but after he kidnaped that nice secretary of Shayne's tonight and boasted to me that he plans to kill her after the funeral tomorrow, I can't remain silent any longer. She is a sweet girl and after seeing her with Charles tonight, I am revolted. Death holds no fears for me. John and Henrietta were old and mean and deserved to die. But this thing tonight is the last straw and I don't want to go on living.' And his name was signed to it," she ended, tears running down her cheeks.

Shayne said, "And my note began: 'I will write this note while I can. I love my sister and have always forgiven her anything she did because I was too weak to protest, but I can't go on . . .' "

He broke off, nodding his head understandingly. "That was the end of a line." He took the note from his pocket and looked at it.

"Fortuitously, the first two words of a line down in

175

the middle of your note were, 'any longer.' By tearing the two notes across between those two lines, the final note read as though the same thought was being carried on . . . with the implication that Marvin intended to kill himself instead of voicing his fear that Charles planned to kill him. Very neat. And so you went along with the deception?"

"What else could I do?" she sobbed frantically. "Charles practically admitted he had killed Marvin, and he threatened to kill me, too, unless I . . ."

"You damned lying bitch!" Charles was sitting upright on the floor with his wrists handcuffed behind him. His eyes were wild and there were bubbles of gray froth on his lips. "I did it all for you, goddam it, after they dug up your lousy dog and I knew they'd find your strychnine in her belly that you'd meant for Henrietta. I told you last night why I grabbed the girl. Because I found the strychnine in your own handbag after you'd put it in Henrietta's chicken to shut her up."

"And I told you I *didn't* do it," she screamed at him, thrusting herself up from the depths of her chair. "I never saw the strychnine and I didn't do anything to John."

Shayne thrust her back into the chair savagely and said, "To hell with all that. You were talking about Lucy Hamilton. *What* did Charles do to her? *Where is she?*"

"In the boathouse. She was in the boathouse last night. But he said . . ."

Shayne whirled away from her and shot out at Petrie and Donovan, "Hold everything as it is." He pounded down the hallway and out through the kitchen door, across the parking lot and past the garage to the path leading to the boathouse at the foot of the cliff.

He plunged recklessly down the wooden stairs, taking

them three at a time, and when he reached the wooden dock at the bottom where he and Rourke had disembarked the preceding night, he saw a padlock on the door of the boathouse.

It was a flimsy-looking door, and he paused in front of it only momentarily before drawing back and lowering his left shoulder, then driving forward with all his strength to hit the door just beside the padlocked hasp.

The weathered wood splintered and gave way, and Shayne stepped through a gaping hole to see a neat Chris-Craft tied fore and aft in front of him with enough slack in the ropes so it could rise and fall with the bay tide.

He found an electric switch beside the smashed door and thumbed it, and an overhead light came on and he saw the figure of a girl huddled forlornly in one corner with a ragged blanket thrown over her.

He took two strides and snatched the blanket away from Lucy Hamilton's body, saw that she was fully clothed, lying on her side with her body drawn into a bow with wrists tied tightly to her ankles, wide strips of adhesive tape tightly over her mouth.

Her eyes were wide open and unblinking, staring up at him, and he dropped to his knees beside her, choking back an oath and telling her cheerfully, "The marines have landed, angel."

He cut the rope binding her wrists to her ankles and eased her back gently onto the rough boards, rubbing the constricted leg muscles and straightening one and then the other slowly and gently so normal circulation would be restored.

Then he crouched over her and grinned down into the wide-open brown eyes while he worked a thumbnail carefully under one end of the overlapping strips of adhesive across her mouth and told her, "This is going

177

to hurt, angel." He placed the wide palm of his other hand firmly on her forehead to hold her head solidly against the floor, got a good grip on the loosened ends of tape and pulled it loose with one strong jerk.

She moaned agonizingly and he felt hot tears against his palm, and he gathered her up in his arms like a little child and held her face tightly against his chest and pressed his lips gently against her disarranged curls and murmured crazy things to her which both of them remembered a long time afterward.

When she was through trembling and through crying and was able to speak in a small voice that was still somewhat distorted by pain, he continued to hold her tightly in his arms and she answered the few questions he needed answers to.

"Are you all *right*, Lucy? You know what I mean?" She whispered, "Yes."

"Who put you here?"

"Charles. He telephoned . . ."

"I don't care how he worked it," Shayne told her brusquely. "Save your breath for important things. Did Charles kill Rogell?"

"I don't think so. He and Marvin . . . talked. He told Marvin Anita did it, and he was doing this to save her."

"Did Marvin believe it?"

"I . . . think so. He was good, Michael. Don't blame Marvin. He was . . . drunk, but decent. He argued with Charles about me. He threatened to tell you. Even after . . . Charles offered me to him. Do you understand? My body. Charles said . . . it wouldn't matter to me because I'd have to die anyway as soon as I'd served my purpose. Oh, my God, Michael!" She shuddered violently and gave way in the circle of his arms to the hysteria which she had been fighting back.

"I've been so frightened," she moaned through strangled sobs against his chest. "Lying here hour after hour. Wondering and waiting . . ."

Shayne's arms tightened around her so her voice was smothered against his body.

Still holding her closely, he got to his feet and carried her out through the smashed wooden door into the sunlight. One arm crept around his neck tightly as he carried her up the stairs and around to the front of the house and his parked car. He opened the rear door and slid her inside gently onto the cushion and said, "Stretch out and try to relax. I'll send the maid out with a glass of water which you should sip on . . . and I'll be ready to drive you home in a few minutes. Think you can hold out?"

She opened her eyes and smiled tremulously up into his concerned face. "I can stand anything now." She let out a little sigh of contentment and her eyelids fluttered shut again.

Chapter nineteen

The tableau hadn't changed much when Shayne came back into the study. Petrie and Donovan stood on guard in the archway, Anita was still huddled in the same chair, and Charles sat on the floor with his wrists handcuffed behind him. Peabody had moved to the bar and was mixing a drink, and Henrietta had taken advantage of his absence to make herself a stiff highball. The lawyer still sat stiffly in his chair, looking as though he very much wished he were some place else.

No one spoke as Shayne walked in between Petrie and Donovan. The big redhead's face was impassive as he strode across the room and stopped directly in front of Charles and looked down at him. The chauffeur tilted back his head to look up with a snarl of defiance, and Shayne leaned down slightly to hit him a full-swinging, open-handed blow on the left cheek.

The sound of the impact was loud in the room, and the force of it knocked Charles sprawling onto his side. Still without speaking, Shayne leaned down farther and savagely jerked him back up to a sitting position, set himself solidly and swung another full-arm blow with his left hand. Charles went over in the other direction like a ninepin and stayed there, and Anita began sobbing wildly in her chair.

Shayne jerked the chauffeur roughly erect again and

said happily, "This is real good fun, Charles. I can keep it up all day without getting tired. You want to start talking?"

"I did it for her," he mumbled. "I knew if you found the strychnine in Daffy you'd be on to her for feeding the same stuff to the old man. I wasn't going to hurt the girl. All I wanted was to scare you off from an autopsy."

"But Marvin messed things up by catching you with Lucy and threatening to turn you in for kidnaping," said Shayne conversationally.

"Even when I *told* him it was just to protect his sister," complained Charles with every appearance of righteous anger. "I couldn't afford that . . . not right then . . . so I tried to scare him out of it. How was I to know the fool was drunk enough to kill himself?"

Shayne said, "I don't believe he was. *You* had the strychnine. Remember? You admitted finding it in Anita's pocketbook after you buried Daffy."

"That's a lousy lie," cried out Anita viciously. "I didn't either. I didn't touch any strychnine. Why would I? If it was in my pocketbook, somebody put it there just to throw suspicion on me."

Shayne paid no attention to her. "But you did have it," he reminded Charles. "How did Marvin get hold of it to commit suicide?"

"I gave it to him, that's why," Charles glared up at him sullenly. "To prove to him that his own sister had tried to poison Henrietta to shut her up. So the fool would get some sense in his head and let me handle it my own way."

Shayne said, "We won't worry too much about whether you fed the stuff to Marvin or he took it himself. Kidnaping is a capital offense and they can only burn you once." He turned away from Charles and went over to the bar where he was pleased to find a bottle of

181

cognac. He poured two inches in a highball glass and drank half of it, smiled pleasantly at the lawyer and told him, "I know you'd like to read that will and get out of here. There's just one small matter to clear up."

He transferred his bland gaze to Henrietta who sat bolt upright in a straight chair, gripping her highball glass tightly in both bony hands.

"You hired me to do a certain job for you yesterday, Miss Rogell. I did it, so I have no intention of returning the retainer you paid me. An autopsy was performed secretly on your brother last night." He held her gaze impassively. "All of you here will be interested to know that John Rogell died of heart failure . . . exactly as Dr. Evans stated on the death certificate."

A long-drawn sigh came from Anita's lips. She sat up straight and her eyes flamed contemptuously at Charles on the floor. "I told you so." Her voice was thin with rage. "But you wouldn't believe me. Your lousy ego made you think I'd done something to John . . . when I loved him all the time."

"See here, young man." Henrietta's heavy voice cut in unexpectedly. "What sort of nincompoop performed that autopsy on my brother?"

"The regular police surgeon. A very competent man."

"Competent, my foot! He's a bungling fool. Didn't he have brains enough to check for digitalis?"

"But it was common knowledge that your brother had been taking digitalis for years," protested Shayne. "He would naturally expect to find that in his system."

"Of course he would. And that's exactly why he should have measured the quantity he swallowed the night he died. Didn't he realize that's exactly what his wife would use to kill him? Instead of strychnine or something obvious like that? Mrs. Blair will bear me out that she knew exactly what effect an overdose would

182

have. Dr. Evans warned her carefully enough. I could have told that fool doctor what to look for."

Shayne nodded and tugged thoughtfully at his left ear lobe. "Yes, I'm sure you could, Miss Rogell. Because you put that extra teaspoonful in his milk yourself, didn't you?"

"Nonsense. It's just that I happen to be the only one around here with a brain in my head."

Shayne shook his red head soberly. "I'm going to arrest you for poisoning your brother, Miss Rogell. And for attempting to frame Anita for your crime by putting strychnine in your own creamed chicken and feeding it to Daffy in a last-ditch effort to draw attention to your first crime."

"Of all the fantastic nonsense I ever heard!" she exclaimed crisply. "And then, I suppose, I came to the best private detective in Miami and hired him to make a case against me?"

"That's exactly what you did. After your scheme to kill Daffy fell flat on its face and she was safely buried with the strychnine inside her. It must have been quite a blow to you when these two detectives who investigated that night didn't even look into Anita's handbag and find the strychnine where you'd put it. Instead, Charles found it there, and unfortunately jumped to the conclusion you'd hoped the detectives would reach."

Henrietta's lips were tightly compressed and she shook her gray head wonderingly from side to side. "And what possible motive would *I* have for doing all those things, Mr. Michael Shayne? You know the provisions of John's will. I'm cut off without a penny of my own. *She* gets it all." She jerked her head indignantly toward Anita. "I was the last person in the world to want to see John in his grave."

"Correction," said Shayne gravely. "You were the

183

only person in this entire household with any motive at all. The others knew they were provided for in his will and could well afford to wait. Even Marvin Dale. Even though Rogell might have kicked him out of his soft spot here, his sister would have continued to provide for him until she came into a lot of millions on her husband's natural death. You were the only one who couldn't afford to wait for that. Your only chance of ever getting your hands on the money you felt was rightfully yours was to arrange it so Anita would be convicted of murdering him. In that case, the will would be set aside because a murderer cannot legally profit by her crime. If you waited for John to die normally, you were sunk. So . . . you didn't wait, Miss Rogell."

"You've got it all worked out, haven't you?" she asked sarcastically. "The one thing you can't show is opportunity. Haven't you brains enough in that red head of yours to realize that I'm the *only* person here who couldn't have dosed John's milk the night he died? All the others had a chance at it. I didn't."

"That," said Shayne heavily, "is why I suspected you from the first. The night it happened was the one night when you had a perfect alibi. That's why you weren't afraid to come to me and hire me to reopen the case. You figured you were perfectly safe. No matter who else might be suspected, it couldn't be you."

"Of all the Alice in Wonderland logic I ever heard," said Henrietta with a sniff, "that takes the cake. Is that the way you solve all your cases, young man? By finding the one person who has a perfect alibi and then suspecting him?"

Shayne grinned ruefully. "It isn't always that easy. But from the beginning in this one it looked as though you might have carefully built yourself an alibi. As though you knew what was going to happen to John

184

that night, and provided yourself with witnesses to prove you couldn't have tampered with the chocolate milk."

"And you'll have to admit I couldn't have," she pointed out with dry satisfaction. "I was in my own room while Mrs. Blair was fixing it. She came straight upstairs after leaving it on the dining table, and I stopped her on the way up and went up to her room with her where I stayed every minute until after he had his attack. You can ask Mrs. Blair."

"I've already asked Mrs. Blair," Shayne countered easily. "She told me the same thing . . . along with some other interesting bits of information."

He turned from Henrietta to the housekeeper who had not spoken a word since he first entered the room. "Do you remember telling me how Charles was in the kitchen that evening and poured out the last glass of milk to drink it with some cookies before you noticed it was the last and had to take it away from him so there'd be the regular cupful for Mr. Rogell?"

"I remember that, Mr. Shayne."

"And you were surprised to discover it was the last glass in the refrigerator?" Shayne pressed on. "You'd thought there was another full bottle, but suddenly discovered there wasn't and that you *had* to have Charles's glass for Mr. Rogell? Do you remember that, too?"

"Yes, I do. I would have sworn there was another full bottle left after I made dinner."

"Did you ever stop to wonder what had become of the bottle you thought was there . . . but wasn't?"

"I don't know. I . . . I guess I didn't think too hard."

"Because you had no reason to think about it at the time," Shayne pointed out soothingly. "You had no reason to suspect that there was going to be a lethal amount of digitalis in his milk that night, so you nat-

185

urally wouldn't suspect that Henrietta had poured out the other bottle after dinner and poured digitalis into the last cup that was left . . . *knowing* that would be the cup you would put into the thermos for Rogell to drink. But now that you think back, Mrs. Blair, don't you *know* there was another bottle that disappeared from the refrigerator before you heated milk for Rogell?"

"You're putting words in her mouth," said Henrietta loudly. "No jury will ever believe her."

Shayne said grimly, "I think they will. Let's wait and see."

Chapter twenty

Lucy Hamilton had luxuriated in a long, soaking, hot bath, and rubbed soothing cold cream on her lips from which Shayne had roughly ripped away the adhesive tape. With make-up carefully applied to offset the deathly pallor of her face and arrayed in her nicest silk dressing gown and most frivolous slippers, she was happily relaxed at one end of the sofa in the security of her own apartment with Michael Shayne lounging at the other end. She had a tinkling highball glass in her hand, and on the glass table in front of the sofa were bottles of whisky and cognac, a carafe of ice water and a bucket of ice cubes. Up to this point, Shayne had not allowed her to do any talking. Now he looked at her sternly over the rim of a wineglass nearly full of cognac, and ordered, "Tell me just how it happened last night."

She said, "I was silly, Michael. I never will forgive myself. But I was worried about you going out to dig up that dog, and when I got the telephone call I didn't stop to think."

He said, "There was a telephone call?"

"About nine o'clock." She took a sip of her drink, then plunged into the recital with downcast eyes.

"I ate dinner alone and came back to wait for some

word from you. I was sitting right here relaxing with a drink and a cigarette when the phone rang. I was so sure it would be you. I ran to the phone and a man's voice answered. He talked fast and I didn't recognize it at all. But he said: 'Miss Hamilton, Mike Shayne gave me this number to call you. He needs you fast. Meet him in his office in fifteen minutes. If he's not there, wait.' Then he hung up before I could ask any questions. What could I do, Michael? I was worried, and all I could think of was that the call must be from you because this number is unlisted and you're about the only one who knows it. So I called a taxi and kicked off my slippers and put on my shoes and hurried out.

"There was a car parked just beyond the office, but I didn't notice it until a man got out as I started across the sidewalk. He called to me and I turned and saw it was Charles. The block was deserted and he grabbed me and dragged me over to his car and shoved me in the front seat and stuck that adhesive over my mouth so I couldn't yell. Then he drove straight out to the house and carried me down to the boathouse and tied me up and left me. All that time he didn't say a single word, Michael. I didn't know what to think.

"It seemed like hours later when he came back. There's a telephone extension in the boathouse, and he took the tape off my mouth and made me call you and told me exactly what to say to you or else he'd kill me right off, and so I said it and then tried to tell you not to pay any attention to me, but he broke the connection.

"And then Anita's brother came stumbling into the boathouse." Her voice trembled momentarily and she paused to take a long drink. "He was obviously drunk, and Charles was enraged when he saw him. Marvin was just drunk enough to exhibit some decent instincts, and he recognized me from yesterday and wanted to know what Charles was doing with me. So Charles told him. That he was doing it all for Anita . . . to prevent you from analyzing the dog and getting an autopsy on Mr. Rogell, which he told Marvin would probably send her to the electric chair.

"Marvin didn't seem much surprised, but he drunkenly insisted that Charles had to let me go. And Charles argued with him. He even suggested that Marvin stay out in the boathouse alone with me all night and have all the fun he wanted because, Charles told him, he would have to kill me anyhow as soon as the funeral was over and the danger to Anita was past.

"But Marvin got very angry and swore he would notify you where I was, and Charles laughed at him and said he'd never get away from the grounds and threatened to kill him if he didn't keep his mouth shut. And they went away still arguing, and left me there, tied up and gagged for what seemed like days until you broke in the door.

"I was very glad to see you, Michael," she ended sedately, her brown eyes dancing at him over the rim of her glass as she tilted it for another long drink.

He said gruffly, "The feeling was mutual." He got out a cigarette and lit it very deliberately, stretched his long legs out in front of him and blew a streamer of blue smoke toward the ceiling.

"There's just one other question, angel," he told her in a deceptively mild voice.

"What is it?"

"You mentioned the fact that your phone is unlisted and you were thrown off guard because only a few people know the number. How do you account for the fact that Charles knew it?"

189

"I was afraid you were going to ask me that, Michael," she said in a very small voice.

He waited a long moment without looking at her. Then he said, "Well?"

"I gave it to him yesterday, Michael. When I . . . when he . . . was showing me Daffy's grave."

"During that 'little moment out there alone under the cypress tree with Charles'?" Shayne quoted to her from her own words yesterday afternoon.

She wet her lips nervously. "Yes. That's when. I don't know what ever came over me."

Shayne said, "Watch it in the future when you're alone in the woods with a man and he makes you feel virginal." He put down his glass and turned to her slowly and he wasn't smiling. In a thick voice he said, "Honest to God, Lucy . . ."

There were tears in her eyes and her swiftly indrawn breath made a little whimpering sound, and then she was in his arms, and after that no word was spoken in the apartment for a long time.

THE DELL GREAT MYSTERY LIBRARY

*Modern masterpieces by
world-famous mystery writers*